W9-BFD-941

THE DRAGON
IN THE
LIBRARY

DRAGON KEEPERS

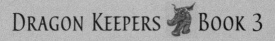

DRAGON KEEPERS 🐉 BOOK 3

THE DRAGON IN THE LIBRARY

KATE KLIMO

with illustrations
by
JOHN SHROADES

A YEARLING BOOK

For Harry

Text copyright © 2010 by Kate Klimo
Cover art and interior illustrations copyright © 2010 by John Shroades

All rights reserved. Published in the United States by Yearling, an imprint of Random House Children's Books, a division of Random House, Inc., New York. Originally published in hardcover in the United States by Random House Children's Books, New York, in 2010.

Yearling and the jumping horse design are registered trademarks of Random House, Inc.

Visit us on the Web! www.randomhouse.com/kids

Educators and librarians, for a variety of teaching tools, visit us at www.randomhouse.com/teachers

The Library of Congress has cataloged the hardcover edition of this work as follows:
Klimo, Kate.
The dragon in the library / Kate Klimo ; with illustrations by John Shroades. — 1st ed.
p. cm. — (Dragon Keepers ; 3)
Summary: Dragon Keepers Jesse and Daisy, along with their dragon, Emmy, must save their friend Professor Andersson from an evil witch, who happens to be St. George the Dragon Slayer's girlfriend.
ISBN 978-0-375-85591-7 (trade) — ISBN 978-0-375-95591-4 (lib. bdg.) — ISBN 978-0-375-89315-5 (ebook)
[1. Dragons—Fiction. 2. Magic—Fiction. 3. Libraries—Fiction. 4. Cousins—Fiction.]
I. Shroades, John, ill. II. Title.
PZ7.K67896Dpl 2010
[Fic]—dc22
2009016592

ISBN 978-0-375-85592-4 (tr. pbk.)

Printed in the United States of America
10 9 8

First Yearling Edition 2011

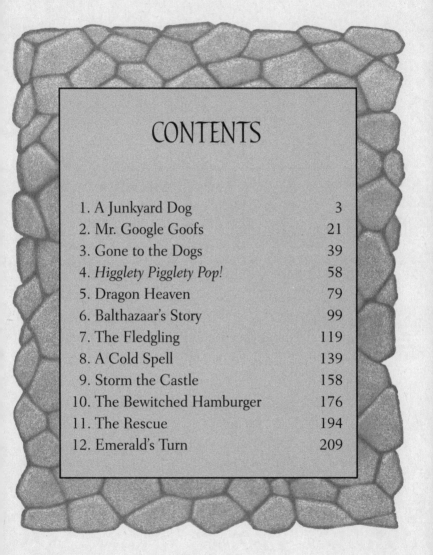

CONTENTS

THE WORLD
IS TALKING TO US.
EVERYTHING IN IT
HAS A STORY TO TELL.
ALL WE HAVE TO DO
IS SIT QUIETLY
AND LISTEN.
THIS STORY BEGINS
IN THE LIBRARY. . . .

CHAPTER ONE

A JUNKYARD DOG

Dear Mom and Dad, We're having a heat
wave. Of course, people in Tanzania would say
it's a cold spell. But it is still way too hot for
sheepdogs. Poor Emmy—all she wants to do
is stay in the garage in the cool dark. Aunt

3

Maggie says she wants to give her a buzz
cut, but Daisy and I say NO WAY!!!!! I am
writing to you from the library computer.
Daisy and I have special privileges here.
That's because we are good about returning
books on time. Plus we get extra credit for
never using the Chicken Box. Bet you don't
know what that is. It's this big old mailbox
outside the front doors. Mr. Stenson, the
librarian, painted it yellow and stuck pictures
of chickens all over it. People who are too
chicken to bring overdue books back to the
librarian's desk drop them off in the Chicken
Box and run for the hills. *Pawk-pawk-pawk-
pawk-pawk!*

Jesse didn't write this, but most of the books
they had taken out lately were really for Emmy to
read *all by herself*. Their pet dragon (who sometimes masked herself as a sheepdog) had taught
herself how to read! Three weeks before, they had
rescued a big, red leather-bound book from St.
George the Dragon Slayer and hidden it in the parlor of their neighbor, Miss Alodie. The size of a
giant coffee table, it was written in a language none
of them could understand. Emmy hoped that if she
became a good enough reader, she would be able to

decode what was written on the book's mysterious pages. So far, they hadn't been able to open the book, much less figure out what it said on the inside.

Jesse felt someone bump his back and he turned around. Daisy had a pile of books balanced beneath her chin. "All set," she said, blowing white-blond wisps of hair off her forehead.

Jesse sent the e-mail to his parents and signed off, then bounced up to put his arms through the backpack. The bag contained a light load of two water bottles and Daisy's wildflower notebook, but it was about to get a lot heavier. Jesse took half of the books from his cousin, and together they went to the librarian's desk.

As always, Mr. Stenson took a lively interest in their picks. "You guys realize you're reading way above your grade level these days?" he asked.

Daisy, three inches taller than Jesse, even though they both were ten years old, jiggled nervously on the balls of her feet. "Well, what do you know about that," she said with a bright smile.

"Wow," Jesse said softly, ducking to hide beneath his mop of shaggy brown hair.

Mr. Stenson reviewed their choices as he passed the books under the scanner. "Looks like you're having an E. Nesbit festival. *Five Children and It, The Story of the Amulet,* and *Dragon Tales.* Next up, *The Phantom Tollbooth,* and—jeepers— look at this one! Howard Pyle's *Twilight Land.* I see you're this dandy old chestnut's first readers in eight years! Next up: *Peter Pan,* and, last but not least, one of my personal faves, *Higglety Pigglety Pop!,* starring a spiffy little terrier. I wonder which spiffy English sheepdog made *this* pick?"

Magically masked as a sheepdog, with her nose pressed to the front door's big glass pane, Emmy pulled back and let out a loud bark.

"Look at her," said Mr. Stenson fondly. "She knows we're talking about her. I bet she's going to have a blast at the Pets Allowed Slumber Party. You kids are coming tomorrow night, aren't you?"

"Of course we are!" Jesse said.

"Wouldn't miss it," Daisy added.

"And I think I can guess which of these books you've chosen to read at the party," Mr. Stenson said with a knowing smile.

The annual slumber party was held at the library for third, fourth, and fifth graders and their pets (so long as they were certified housebroken and thoroughly well-behaved). One of the highlights of the party was before bedtime, when each guest read a chapter from a book about an animal. The only restriction Mr. Stenson had placed on the selection was that it couldn't be scary. "No fair scaring the bejeepers out of the librarians," he had said. This year, for the first time, Jesse and Daisy actually had an animal to bring and not just a book about one. Meanwhile, however, something was causing that pet to bark her furry head off.

Mr. Stenson slid the stack of books toward the cousins and nodded in Emmy's direction. "She sounds plenty eager to me."

Jesse and Daisy frowned at each other. Didn't that barking sound a little less like eager and a lot more like distressed? They turned around to see what the trouble was.

A woman they didn't recognize was depositing a book in the Chicken Box. She screamed as Emmy lunged at her very small dog. The woman yanked her dog back as it strained at the leash, its eyes bulging out of its bony little skull. Emmy, whose leash was tied to one leg of the Chicken Box, pulled against it so frantically, Jesse was afraid she would tear herself loose. A small crowd of people stood on the steps of the library and watched the face-off with a mixture of amusement and fear.

Mr. Stenson lifted the telephone and punched in a number. "Nothing personal to Emmy but it's times like this I'm glad we're next door to the pound," he said.

Jesse's eyes went wide. "You're calling Ms. Mindy?"

"Darn tootin', I am," Mr. Stenson said cheerily, just as the growling outside exploded into all-out warfare.

Jesse and Daisy tore out the door and pulled Emmy off the little dog just as Ms. Mindy dashed over from next door, armed with a net.

Ms. Mindy eyed the canine culprits with suspicion. "Okay," she said, "which one of you furry troublemakers started this? Am I gonna have to finish it for you?"

Jesse had only one thought in his head, and that was *If this lady messes with our dog, she'll turn back into a dragon.* "No! Everything's fine now," he said, shielding Emmy in case Ms. Mindy's zapper finger got a little itchy.

"It's just too hot to be a sheepdog," Daisy said to Ms. Mindy.

"The little yappy one started it," somebody in the crowd said, and there was a murmur of agreement.

The little yappy one's owner said, "Spencer was just trying to make nicey-nice."

"Ma'am?" the dogcatcher said to the owner. "I'm going to have to ask you and Spencer to move along now, please. Everybody," she said to the others, "show's over. Get back to your lives."

Jesse went back inside to pack up their books while Daisy stayed with Emmy, holding her head and crooning in her ear. Jesse came out, bent beneath the weight on his back. They shared backpack duty, and today was his turn to carry it.

Ms. Mindy stepped in close to Jesse and Daisy and said in a low voice, "Kids, whatever you do, don't let your dog run around loose today, okay?"

Jesse and Daisy nodded.

"How come?" Jesse asked.

Ms. Mindy said, "Somebody broke into the pound last night."

"Whoa!" said Daisy.

"Let out every dog in the place," Ms. Mindy said, "when we were at maximum capacity. Which means there are now about three dozen dogs at liberty in this town."

"Who let them loose?" Daisy asked.

Ms. Mindy looked to the right and to the left, as if spies might be listening. "Not a clue. All I know is there are some mighty big dogs at large."

"How come you're not out catching them?" Jesse asked.

Ms. Mindy threw up both hands. "I've been at it since dawn. Had to come in to change. Sweated right through my uniform. I've been everywhere and back again, and I haven't seen a one of them," she said.

"Holy moly!" said Daisy.

"Holy moly is right, young lady," Ms. Mindy said. "You three take care now."

Jesse and Daisy crept down the steps of the library and headed home. Technically, it was Daisy's home, but Jesse had been living there since before the summer started. His parents were doctors in Africa running a children's clinic. He had traveled all over the world with them since he was born, but now he wanted to live in America for a while. Since he had spent every summer with his cousins, Uncle Joe, and Aunt Maggie, this was his second home. Now that her much bigger brothers, Aaron and Noah, had grown up and moved away, Daisy was especially happy not to be the only kid left at home.

Neither Jesse nor Daisy said very much on the walk home. It was too hot to talk, and both wanted to keep an eye out for big dogs running around loose. They let out a sigh of relief when they stepped into the cool, damp, dark garage and closed the door behind them.

Emmy shook herself all over and unmasked into her dragon form. The cousins were startled anew at how big she had gotten in a few short weeks. She was now as big as a medium-size elephant. When she drew herself up high on her haunches, the cousins had to crane their necks to meet her eye.

"Do you mind explaining what happened back there?" Jesse asked Emmy.

"Yeah," said Daisy. "Why couldn't you just make nicey-nice?"

"Because maybe I am not nicey-nice," Emmy griped.

"Yes, you are!" Daisy said. "You're a very nice dragon. Most of the time."

"Emmy, do you know what Ms. Mindy had?" Jesse told her. "A zapper thingie. She might have zapped you into a dragon in front of the whole town!"

Emmy sulked. "It wasn't my fault. I didn't do anything. That creepy little rat dog sniffed me."

"Emmy, sniffing is not a good reason to fight," said Daisy.

Emmy smoldered with indignation. "He sniffed my butt!"

Daisy rolled her eyes.

"That's what dogs do, Emmy; you know that," Jesse said, unloading the books from the backpack and stacking them on the old picnic table next to Emmy's nest. Just as she had outgrown the sock drawer, she had outgrown her other nest in the old wooden packing crate filled with rolled-up socks. A week before, they had sawed off the sides of two crates and nailed them together to make one big nest. It was a good thing their grandmother sent them each a pair of socks every week because the new crate needed an awful lot of them to make the nest as cozy as the old one.

Daisy said to Emmy, "Dogs sniff each other's butts all the time. It's how they say hello. It's time you got used to it."

"It was okay when I was a baby, but it is not okay now. Because that is *not* how dragons say hello," Emmy said huffily. She went over to the table, picked up the first book on the pile—which happened to be *The Book of Dragons*—and climbed into her nest.

"How *do* dragons say hello?" Daisy asked.

With one dark green, sickle-shaped talon, Emmy carefully opened the book to the first page. "I don't know," she said primly. "Maybe Mrs. Nesbit will tell me how in this book of hers that I am going to read now, *if* my bossy-pants Keepers will let me be."

The cousins watched, impressed, as Emmy's eyes ran down the first page and up to the top of the next. Not only was she a good reader, she was lightning fast. Why, they wondered, was she so cranky these days?

"You're not a happy dragon, are you, Emmy?" said Jesse.

Emmy heaved a big sigh. "No, Jesse Tiger. I am not a happy dragon," she said.

"It's the heat," said Daisy.

Without looking up from her book, Emmy said evenly, "Dragons can fly into the craters of live volcanoes."

"Well, then, what is it? Is there something you need that you're not getting?" Jesse asked.

Emmy nodded.

"Then tell us what it is," said Daisy, "and we'll try really hard to get it for you."

"I need . . ." Emmy stared off into space while the cousins waited. *"Something,"* she said, shrugging and turning back to her book.

Jesse sagged. "Okay, but what is the *something*?" he said.

Emmy blinked twice. "Beats me."

"Are you hungry?" said Daisy. "You didn't finish your eggshell omelet this morning. Maybe you're peckish."

"Maybe I am," said Emmy, sounding every bit as puzzled as they were.

"Then what would you like?" said Jesse.

Emmy was silent. *"Something?"* she said after a bit.

Jesse counted to ten very slowly.

Daisy clapped her hands. "I've got it! How about a Snowy Woods?" It was their name for cream cheese smeared on raw broccoli stalks, a frequent snack request from Emmy.

Emmy shook her head.

"A Double Swiss Delight?" Jesse suggested. This, surely, was her all-time favorite brunch food: Swiss cheese melted on crunchy leaves of Swiss chard.

Emmy got an ornery glint in her eye. "You mean Double Swiss Doo-doo Pie? I am not a baby anymore, you two."

"No, you're not," said Jesse. Out of the corner of his mouth, he said to Daisy, "What she is, is a junkyard dog."

"Junkyard dog" was what Jesse's mother called anyone who got up on the wrong side of the bed, or, in this case, crate.

Daisy was about to offer up another snack suggestion when Jesse said, "Never mind, Em. We'll fix you something really yummy and surprise you."

Grabbing the backpack, Daisy followed Jesse out of the garage. They locked the door behind them, as always.

Daisy banged her head softly and repeatedly against the door. "What. Exactly. Is. Her. Basic. *Problem?*"

Jesse shook his head wearily. "Is it me, or has she been like this for *weeks*?"

Daisy dug her wildflower notebook out of the pack. She had marked off a section in the back for keeping track of Emmy's size, food preferences, and moods. She counted ten frowny faces in a row and said, "A week and a half, to be exact. Ten days straight of serious attitude," she said. "But it feels more like ten *years*. That yummy surprise better be good."

"Well," Jesse said, "I was thinking we did have brussels sprouts for dinner last night."

Daisy perked up. "Right! A Brussels Sprouts Smoothie. Her favorite beverage! If that doesn't cheer her up, nothing will. What in the world's gotten into her?"

Jesse stopped at the foot of the back steps. "I don't know," he said, "but I sure hope it doesn't have anything to do with her getting bigger."

"You mean, like, the bigger she gets, the grumpier she gets?" Daisy shuddered. "Let's hope not."

On that rather ominous note, Jesse and Daisy walked through the mudroom into the kitchen.

They were surprised to find Uncle Joe sorting rocks on the table instead of in the Rock Shop, the garden shed he had converted into a geology lab. Daisy was even more surprised to find that the small portable TV was switched on in the middle of the day.

"Hi, guys," he said. "Don't turn on the light. It's hotter than Hades in here, but not half as hot as it was out in my shop."

The house did not have air-conditioning, but it did have fans buzzing away in every room. A ceiling fan wheeled slowly overhead, casting long, slow shadows around the room. Uncle Joe wore a tank shirt and shorts, and his long, graying ponytail was bunched into a messy bun.

"What's with the TV?" Daisy asked.

"There was a special on about the North Pole," he said with an embarrassed shrug. "I thought it might cool me off."

Jesse got the container of leftover brussels sprouts and some sour cream out of the refrigerator. Daisy set the ice dispenser on the freezer door to Crush and filled a bowl with ice chips. Jesse dumped the ingredients into the blender and Daisy added the ice. Daisy went to the refrigerator to get the secret ingredient: applesauce. She set it on the counter next to the blender. Then she climbed onto the back rungs of her father's chair.

"So what's on now, Poppy?" she asked.

"One of those trendy dog-trainer shows," said Uncle Joe, sliding a sparkly blue-black rock from one pile to the next. "It's called *Top Dog*. Our dynamic hostess, Ms. Sadie Huffington, says 'Bring me your vicious dogs and I'll train them to be meek as lambs.' She's something else."

While Jesse worked the blender, Daisy watched the TV. A tall, beautiful woman with flowing red hair and high black boots held a long switch in her hand. She looked more like a lion tamer than a dog trainer. The camera closed in on a Doberman pinscher. It lunged at the camera, saliva dripping from its jaws. Then the camera pulled back to Sadie Huffington, who stood over the big dog, snapping the switch smartly against her boot. The ferocious-looking Doberman sank to the floor and whimpered. She snapped the switch again and the dog rolled over onto its back and practically mewed like a kitten.

"How'd she do that?" Daisy asked.

"Just look him dead in the eye and never let your steady gaze waver," said Sadie Huffington into the camera, as if in direct reply to Daisy. "It's easy!" She smiled. Her lipstick was gleaming red, her teeth were large and white, and her eyes were an eerie yellowish green. "So long as they know who's Top Dog!"

"Hmm," said Daisy as an ad for flea powder came on.

"It's the patented *Top Dog* Ten-Yard Stare that does it," Uncle Joe said. "Too bad I didn't have one of those to keep you and your big brothers in line, eh?" He grinned.

"Oh, Poppy!" Daisy said with a roll of her eyes.

"All set," Jesse said as he rinsed out the blender jar and set it to drain on the rack.

"See you later," Daisy told her father.

"What about lunch?" he called after them.

"Too hot to eat," Daisy said over her shoulder.

"I know what you mean," her father said.

Daisy opened the garage door and Jesse made a dramatic entrance. "Ta-da!" he said, holding the tall frosted glass up high. He had garnished it with a sprig of mint and had even stuck two straws in it. He carried the glass over to Emmy and held it to her lips. The cousins watched as Emmy opened her bright pink mouth, fastened her lips around the straw, and nearly emptied the glass in one long, noisy slurp.

"Ptoooie!" Emmy spat out the smoothie—and both straws, too—all over the garage floor.

Daisy and Jesse looked down at themselves.

They were spattered with smelly green goo. It was just like the first day of Emmy's life, when they had tried to feed her all sorts of food from the refrigerator and she had spat everything out. It had been cute then. It was not cute now.

"I'll get the mop," Daisy said. "You get the hose, Jess."

"You hate me," Emmy said in a dull voice when they had finished hosing down themselves and the garage floor.

"We don't hate you," Daisy said between clenched teeth. "We just wish we knew what was the *matter* with you."

"Does anything hurt?" Jesse asked.

"Yes," Emmy said with a firm little nod.

"What hurts?" Daisy asked eagerly.

Emmy was silent.

"I know," said Jesse with a mirthless smile. "*Something*, right?"

Emmy nodded.

"I've got a great idea," said Daisy under her breath to Jesse. "Let's ask the professor."

"Plan," said Jesse.

After locking Emmy in with her book, they went back into the house and upstairs. They changed out of their wet clothes and met in Jesse's bedroom. Jesse switched on his computer and logged on to www.foundadragon.org. Daisy pulled up a chair next to Jesse as the face of their white-haired dragon consultant appeared on the screen.

Since Professor Andersson had upgraded his site only a couple of weeks before, it was like watching him on a two-way color TV. Wherever his studio was, he looked cool and calm in his crisp white shirt, dapper red bow tie, and dark suit. Maybe it was as hot where he was as it was in Gold-mine City, because he had trimmed his long white beard into a spiffy goatee.

"Greetings!" Professor Andersson said, hailing them with upraised arms. "I was hoping you two would come calling today. There's a matter of grave importance I need to discuss with you."

CHAPTER TWO

MR. GOOGLE GOOFS

"There's a matter of grave importance we need to discuss with you, too," said Jesse.

Daisy got right down to it. "Emmy's been just terrible lately," she said.

The professor looked mildly amused. "I wonder

if one of you would be so good as to define 'terrible' for me?" he asked.

"Grumpy," Daisy said.

"Gloomy," Jesse said.

"Grouchy," Daisy added.

"A junkyard dog," said Jesse.

"A regular snapdragon, in other words," said the professor, enjoying a good chuckle.

Daisy didn't see what was so funny. She asked, "Could Emmy be teething? My nephew gets really grumpy when he's getting a new tooth."

"Dragons don't generally make a fuss when they are cutting teeth," said the professor. "And besides, she should have sufficient dentition to hold her for the next two years, I daresay."

"Is it the summer, then?" Jesse asked. "It's been pretty hot here."

"I doubt it," said the professor. "The metabolism of your dragon is such that she is capable of withstanding furnacelike temperatures."

"That's kind of what she already told us," said Daisy. "My mother wants to cut her sheepdog fur."

"DO NOT LET HER!" the professor thundered. The long white hair on his head seemed to crackle with intensity.

Daisy winced. "Don't worry. I'm just saying—"

"Eighty-seven percent of a dragon's magical

potency rests in its scales," the professor said, in a slightly less thunderous tone. "Since her fur corre-lates to her scales . . . well, I don't need to spell it out for you, do I?"

"No," Daisy said.

"Could it be a bug?" Jesse asked.

The professor frowned, hooking his thumbs in his suspenders and leaning back in his chair. "An infestation of some sort?"

"I mean a *germ* . . . like the dragon flu," Jesse said, "or a summer cold."

The professor shook his head. "Dragons don't ail the way humans do. Their bodies, as a rule, are in superb balance," he said.

"Then why is she in such a crummy mood!" Daisy nearly shouted.

The professor raised an eyebrow. "One might well ask the same question of you, young lady."

Daisy shrugged and sighed. "Point taken," she said.

The professor went on. "I'm afraid you'll just have to be patient with her. Humor her in the meantime, and hope for the best."

Jesse stared at the screen. "That's it?" he said.

"That's all the advice you can give us?" Daisy said. "Wait and hope for the best?"

The cousins turned and stared at each other.

Was this the way it was going to be?

Jesse said, "If you ask me, we're not Dragon Keepers, we're more like Dragon *Slaves*."

"Oh, piffle," said the professor. "Forgive me, dear children, but have I ever given you to believe that being a Dragon Keeper was an unadulterated lark?"

"Whatever *that* means," Jesse muttered.

The professor went on. "Dragon Keeping isn't an amusement, my dears. You are your dragon's Keepers, in good moods and in bad. And that is the way of it, I'm afraid. There's really nothing to be done, unless—" He broke off and furrowed his brow, drumming his fingernails on the desktop.

"Unless what?" Jesse asked, leaning toward the screen.

"Unless . . . ," the professor said. Then he shook his head quickly. "No. No matter how precocious your dragon has shown herself to be, such a thing would be utterly unheard of in the annals of early dragonhood development. Forget it."

"Thanks a bunch," Daisy said through gritted teeth.

"I *will* tell you this," said the professor, holding up a finger. "Valerian."

"What's that?" asked Jesse.

"It's an herb," said Daisy.

"Quite right, young lady," said the professor. "Known to be of use in the calming of fretful canines."

"But Emmy's a dragon," Jesse reminded him.

"Of course she is, my fine young fellow, but when she is in her masked state, you have but to offer her a steaming bowl of valerian tea . . . and her disposition will most likely improve. That is what you are looking for, isn't it? Some measure of relief?"

"I guess," said Jesse doubtfully. "So what was the grave matter you wanted to talk to us about?"

The professor snapped his fingers. "Ah, yes! I wanted to tell you . . ." He leaned across the desk, his dark eyes suddenly fierce beneath white bristling brows. "Beware, Dragon Keepers!"

"Huh," said Jesse, too baffled at first to feel fearful.

Daisy asked, "Beware of *what*?"

Jesse said, "Queen Hap, the hobgoblin queen, stuck St. George in amber like a bug. You said it would be almost impossible to get him out. So what's so scary?"

"St. George does not represent the sole threat to your dragon. Threats to dragons abound, and I sense impending danger," the professor said somberly.

"What's *impending*?" Jesse whispered to Daisy. Daisy shrugged.

"Trouble amasses on the horizon; I feel it in my very marrow," the professor said. "Until further notice, consider yourselves on red alert, Dragon Keepers."

With a heavy sigh, Jesse switched off the computer, and then they headed down the block to Miss Alodie's house. If anyone had valerian tea, they decided, it would be Miss Alodie. They didn't even bother stopping in the garage to collect Emmy. She hadn't been to Miss Alodie's house in over a week. Their newly sprouted, moody-as-all-get-out Nest Potato had no interest in anything but reading.

"What kind of a threat do you think the professor was talking about?" Daisy asked.

"I don't know," said Jesse sullenly. "Maybe there isn't any."

"What do you mean?" said Daisy.

"Maybe the professor's feeling grouchy, too," said Jesse. "Maybe he's just imagining things."

Daisy nodded thoughtfully. The professor had a tendency to express himself dramatically, but she was pretty sure that if the professor felt something in his *very marrow*, the threat was real.

When they got to Miss Alodie's house, they didn't see her in the front garden. So they headed down the side yard path, which was lined by ranks of sturdy sunflowers, towering at least eight feet high. Unnoticed, the sunflowers' big pie-plate faces turned and slowly tracked the cousins as they passed.

There was no Miss Alodie in the back garden, either, where her cutting beds stretched a quarter of an acre to the high hedge of myrtle that ran along the back of her yard. But the garden doors in the rear of the cottage stood wide open. The next moment, Miss Alodie came bursting through them, waving a flowered hanky over her head, as if in surrender.

"Cousins!" she cried. Her green beanie was askew, and fine white hairs stood up around her head in a trembling nimbus. "It's *gone!*"

"What's gone?" Jesse and Daisy chorused.

"Our project. Our prize! The big book!" she cried. "It's gone! Disappeared!"

Jesse and Daisy followed her into the cottage. The small, cozy parlor, normally as neat as a pin, looked as if a cyclone had hit it, leaving lamps overturned, vases dumped, and knickknacks scattered in its wake. The big, red leather-bound book, which sat between the couch and the easy chairs disguised as a coffee table, was gone.

"What happened?" Jesse asked.

"Not five minutes ago, I was out front, thinning my zinnia patch, when I heard all hullabaloo break out inside. I ran in the house and . . ." She pointed to the spot where the book had been.

"Who took it?" Daisy asked.

"Well, not St. George, we know that much. He's out of circulation, for a while at least," Miss Alodie said. She plopped down on the sofa. "But who, then? *Who?*"

The cousins perched on either side of her and pondered the question in uneasy silence.

Then Jesse said, "The professor said we should be on red alert. Maybe this was why."

Miss Alodie snorted. "Well, he might have warned me. I would have stayed inside with the book. I could have thinned the zinnias another day." She pounded her fists on her thighs. "Oh, why am I blaming him? It's my fault. The book was in my care."

Daisy patted Miss Alodie's shoulder. "It's not your fault, either. And we'll get it back, won't we, Jess?"

"Sure, we will," Jesse said, not very convincingly.

Then Daisy remembered the reason for their visit. "Do you have some valerian tea?"

Miss Alodie gave Daisy an odd look.

"It's for Emmy," Daisy said. "The professor pre-scribed it . . . for relief of her grumpiness."

"It so happens I have a formidable valerian blend, if I do say so myself. I'll put the kettle on." Miss Alodie popped up from the sofa and darted into the kitchen. "I'll brew you a pot and put it in a thermos."

By the time Jesse and Daisy had finished tidy-ing the parlor, the steeped tea had deepened to a golden color and Miss Alodie was pouring it into the thermos.

"It has a bit of a kick," Miss Alodie said.

"What do you mean by that?" Jesse asked.

"It might knock her out cold," Miss Alodie said.

"For how long?" Daisy asked as she tucked the thermos into the pack on Jesse's back.

Miss Alodie frowned. "A few minutes, an hour, it depends. You'll need some of these, as well." She handed Daisy a tin, which she pried open. Jesse poked his nose in and sniffed the small spicy-smelling, half-moon-shaped cookies. He reached in.

"Tut-tut! You're not a dog!" Miss Alodie said, tapping his wrist. "These would be my Rock-'em, Sock-'em Dog Biscuits, my son. Home-baked from my own special recipe. To be used only in dire cir-cumstances."

"Dire?" Jesse echoed.

"Absolutely desperate," Miss Alodie said, her blue eyes narrowing with meaning.

Daisy added the tin of dog biscuits to the backpack. They were at the front door when Miss Alodie chirped, "I nearly forgot!" She clambered up the steep staircase that led to the upper floor and trotted back down a minute later holding what looked like a brightly colored tangle of yarn. She divided up the pile and handed some to each of them. "My modest attempt at crochet," she said. "A bit lumpy, but serviceable, I trust. Wear them in good health."

"Thanks," said Jesse and Daisy, examining the odd wad of yarn in their hands.

"What are they?" Daisy asked.

"Why, earmuffs, of course!" said Miss Alodie.

"Earmuffs," Daisy said slowly. "In August. How . . . *useful!*"

"You never know when a heat wave will give way to a cold spell, do you?" Miss Alodie said brightly. "If I were you, I'd keep them handy."

Miss Alodie's gifts, odd as they seemed, had certainly come in handy in the past.

"We will," said Daisy as she stuffed the earmuffs into the backpack's side pouch. "And we'll let you know what the professor says about the book."

Miss Alodie stood in the doorway, looking

suddenly very grave. "Remember, children, when in doubt, look to the collections," she called after them.

Jesse waited until they were on the sidewalk before he said, "What was she talking about? What collections?"

"Our Museum of Magic collections, what else?" Daisy said.

"I didn't realize we had more than one," Jesse said, but he let it go.

On the short walk home, they agreed not to say anything to Emmy about the missing book. There was no use stoking her grouchiness with bad news.

When they got home and went to the garage, Emmy had just begun the second book on the pile. She barely looked up when they came in. Jesse took off the backpack and pulled out the thermos.

"We have something for you," Daisy said. "Something very good for you to drink."

"I will just go 'ptoooie' again," said Emmy with a little sigh. "And then you will hate me."

"We aren't going to hate you, because we could never hate you, and besides, you're not going to spit it out," said Daisy carefully. "This is tea that will help you feel better."

Emmy looked up and narrowed her green eyes. "Who says?"

The cousins exchanged a look of exasperation. They turned back to Emmy. "We say," they chimed.

"Your Dragon Keepers," Jesse added.

"Miss Alodie says so, too," Daisy said. "She brewed it up, especially for you."

"She did?" Emmy leaped out of her nest and bounded over to them. "In that case, I will drink every drop."

"That's the spirit," said Jesse.

"This is special tea," said Daisy, unscrewing the thermos top. "It only makes you better if you drink it when you're in dog form."

Emmy pulled back, her eyes darkening.

"Miss Alodie says," Jesse said.

Emmy burst out, "I DON'T CARE WHAT MISS ALODIE SAYS. I refuse to be a mangy-haired, butt-sniffing, leg-lifting, damp-nosed sheepdog ever, ever, *ever* again!" She turned her back on them and practically wiped them out with a sweep of her tail.

The cousins looked at each other and frowned, fists clenched at their sides.

Daisy waited until her temper had simmered. Then she said, "All right, Emmy. We weren't going to tell you this, because we didn't want to upset you . . . but somebody stole the book."

Emmy swung back around, her tail coming

down on the concrete floor with a loud smack. "Who took it? Did St. George take it?"

"Now, don't go getting all riled up," said Jesse, making calming motions with his hands.

"We don't know yet who took the book," said Daisy.

"But I want it!" Emmy wailed. "And I haven't visited it for days!" A fat tear formed in her right eye and slid down her nose, followed by another and another.

Daisy sighed and went to get a beach towel. Emmy might not be a baby anymore, but she could still cry like one. Daisy handed the towel up to Emmy. "Please don't cry," she said, patting Emmy's flank. "We'll get the book back."

"H-h-how will we do that?" Emmy said tremulously, blowing her nose into the towel with a loud honk.

"Dragon magic!" Daisy said.

Jesse gave Daisy two big thumbs-up signs.

Emmy lowered the beach towel slowly. "Really?"

"What else?" said Daisy. "But first you have to do like Miss Alodie says and drink this tea."

"In your dog form," Jesse added.

Emmy nodded and promptly masked into a sheepdog.

Daisy tipped the thermos and filled the lid with the hot, steaming tea. She set it down on the floor in front of Emmy, who lapped it up neatly with her forked pink tongue. Then she looked up and gave the little yap that meant "More!"

"Did she say how much we're supposed to give her?" Daisy asked Jesse.

Jesse said, "The professor said a bowl. . . ."

But before they could decide, Emmy turned around three times, lay down with her head on her paws, and started snoring softly.

"I guess that's the kick Miss Alodie was talking about," Jesse said.

"It works for me," said Daisy. "Let's go talk to the professor."

Letting their sleeping dog lie, they locked her in the garage and went upstairs to the computer. Jesse typed in the professor's Web address and pressed Return. They waited for the professor's site to come up. Jesse tapped his foot and hummed softly to himself. It seemed to take longer than usual, but eventually, with a great deal of grinding and whirring, the page appeared.

This is what they saw: Professor Andersson's empty chair behind the desk, its leather back turned toward them as if he had spun around and leaped from it in a great hurry.

"Maybe he had to make an emergency trip to the bathroom?" Jesse suggested.

In nervous silence, they waited for the professor to come back.

"Maybe he had to run an errand?" Daisy said.

They waited a bit more, their uneasiness mounting. Then, through the computer speaker, they heard a door slam so loudly, they both jumped. Jesse and Daisy saw a figure enter the studio and perch on the front of the desk, so close to the screen that Jesse couldn't quite make out who it was. But one thing they knew for certain. It wasn't the professor!

The person on-screen settled farther back on the desk. It was a woman! A woman with long, fiery red hair.

"There you are!" She stared at Jesse, right out of the computer monitor, as if he were the one she had been looking for.

Jesse felt a sudden sinking feeling in his chest. *Why me?*

"Well, now, are you going to tell me where he is, or are you going to be a silly little pooch and hold out on me? Come, now. Where is he?" she asked. Her voice had a sizzling quality, and her strange yellow-green eyes bored into him.

Jesse swallowed dryly and said, "Who?"

"You know very well who," she said, her eyes narrowing to slits.

"Oh! The professor?" Jesse asked. "We were wondering the same thing, weren't we, Daze?"

"Don't look in her eyes," Daisy whispered, delivering a sharp elbow to Jesse's ribs. But it was too late for Jesse.

"The professor!" The woman threw back her head and laughed, showing the long white column of her throat. "I know exactly where that useless old hound dog is! It is St. George the Dragon Slayer I seek! Where is he? Tell me. *Now.*"

"Holy moly," Daisy said under her breath.

"W-w-we don't know," Jesse stammered, which was the truth. Only Her Royal Lowness, Queen Hap, knew where St. George was, somewhere beneath the Deep Woods, imprisoned in a giant cube of amber.

"Knave!" she shouted and brought her long switch down on the desk with a sharp *thwop.*

"Honest!" Jesse squeaked from around the knuckles crammed into his mouth. "We really and truly don't know where he is."

Her eyes dug into him. She whispered, "You might as well tell me now, because I will gladly beat it out of you."

Jesse was heartily glad he didn't know where

St. George was, because if he did, he'd have told her for sure. It wasn't the threat of getting beaten. It was something about her eyes. He was vaguely aware of Daisy crawling around on the floor by his feet. The next minute, the screen turned white, then just as suddenly, it went black. Jesse looked down.

Daisy sat on her heels with the computer plug in her hand. Jesse pulled his fingers out of his mouth and wiped the drool off on his sleeve. "Thanks," he said. "What a scary lady!"

"She's Top Dog," said Daisy.

"You're telling *me*," Jesse said with a nervous laugh.

"No, I mean that's who she is," Daisy said. "Don't you remember? She was on that TV show Poppy was watching this afternoon: *Top Dog*. She trains mean dogs to mind her. Her name is Sadie Huffington."

"Oh," said Jesse. "I guess I was busy smashing up the brussels sprouts."

Daisy plugged the computer back in and sat in her chair. "Google Sadie Huffington, Jess," she told him, punching him lightly on the arm.

Jesse nodded and obeyed, waiting for the home page to return. When it did, he keyed "Sadie Huffington" into the Google search box. He expected the usual screen of lists to show itself. But instead he got: "Did you mean 'Uffington'?"

Jesse groused. "No, I did not mean 'Uffington.' I hate when Mr. Google does that," he said. He mashed down the keys, repeating the request for "Sadie Huffington." "Try again."

This time, the computer skipped directly to another site altogether. The scarlet banner across the top of the screen proclaimed: "UFFINGTON CASTLE."

Jesse pounded the computer table and said, "Come on, Googleheimer! Quit messin' with my head."

He was just about to click the cursor on the little red X in the corner to close the page when Daisy put her hand on his arm and said, "Wait, Jess. Maybe we should stay. Maybe this is the site we're meant to see. Read it."

CHAPTER THREE

GONE TO THE DOGS

"How does this help us find the professor?" Jesse said.

"It's a lead," Daisy said. "We're following a lead."

"A lead? What does *that* mean?" Jesse asked.

"Beats me," Daisy said. "But that's what detectives say when they're trying to track down a missing person. The professor is a missing person. So we have to follow leads. Maybe this is one of them. Read."

Jesse read the text on the screen aloud while Daisy paced before the fan.

"'Located in the south of England, Uffington Castle was a double-walled hill fort in the Bronze Age with timber box ramparts that were riveted with sarsen stones at a later period.'" Jesse paused. "Whatever the Sam Hill *that* means."

"I think that just means it's old," Daisy said, continuing to pace. "Keep going."

"Okay. Let's see. It says 'In the last Roman period, around the third century AD, there is evidence for considerable activity on the site, including ritual shafts, animal bones, and coins—'"

"What's a ritual shaft?" Daisy cut in.

Jesse shrugged. "Beats me. The site doesn't say." In the photograph, Uffington Castle was nothing but a pile of timeworn stones. But a modern-day artist's rendering showed what the castle might have looked like once. It was a simple structure in the shape of a triangle: one large, round stone tower flanked by wooden ramparts, each leading to a smaller tower. It reminded him of some of the hilltop castles in southern France his parents had taken him to.

"Look, Daze." He got up and pulled her back to the computer. She glanced at the screen, and Jesse pointed to the main tower. "That's called the keep. It's also called the donjon."

"You mean the dungeon," Daisy said. "I thought dungeons were supposed to be down in the basement."

Jesse shook his head. "That's what everybody thinks, but they usually put prisoners up in the biggest tower so they could keep an eye on them. Those holes in the donjon are called squint holes. They're for looking outside at the approaching enemy. The bigger holes on the bottom of the ramparts are called murder holes. Isn't that cool?"

"Ugh!" said Daisy. "Not! Keep going." She returned to her pacing.

"Soldiers shot arrows through them. Or dumped boiling oil or hot sand down on the enemy."

"That is horrible!" Daisy said, stopping in her tracks. "You're right. This isn't helping us find the professor, Jess."

"But wait, Daze," said Jesse. "You're missing the best part. The garderobe."

"What about it?" she said without enthusiasm.

"The potty!" said Jesse, chuckling. "This one was over the moat, so pee and poop went right into the water."

"Ew! Castles are gross!" Daisy said. "And we're wasting time now."

Castles weren't so much gross, in Jesse's opinion, as they had been built to impress. Inside, there was never any neat stuff, like suits of armor or spears or tapestries. All of that had been moved to museums. Still, it was enough for him just to stand within the dank, dripping rock walls, with all the pigeon poop, and imagine everything that had once gone on there.

On the screen, something caught Jesse's eye. Outside the wall of the castle was a little hill. It was labeled DRAGON HILL. Jesse moved the cursor over and clicked on the link. A new screen came up, and his heart began to beat a little harder as he read aloud the heading set in a medieval typeface: "'The Legend of St. George and the Dragon.'"

Daisy flew back to her chair. "What? Where?" she said.

"This. Here," he said, pointing to the screen.

Now Daisy read aloud: "'The most famous legend of St. George is of him slaying a dragon. In the Middle Ages, dragons represented the devil.'" Daisy sneered. "Boo. Hiss. Who are these people, anyway? I don't like them." But she read on.

"'The village was terrorized by a dragon who lived in a cave in a nearby hillside. The dragon would come out at night and devour all the sheep and cows.'"

"Jeez!" said Jesse. "Don't these people know anything? Dragons don't eat sheep and cows. They eat broccoli and cabbage."

Frowning deeply, Daisy continued: "'Desperate, the king began to sacrifice maidens every full moon, until only the king's daughter, the royal Princess Sadra, remained.' Look, Jess," she said, pointing to a series of old tapestries on the screen. "Does this look like anyone we know?"

Jesse looked and his jaw dropped. Princess Sadra had long red hair and pale skin. And although he couldn't tell what color her eyes were, he began to get the same sinking feeling in his chest, so he looked away.

Daisy read faster now. "'The king said that anyone who could slay the dragon would be rewarded with the hand of his daughter. St. George heard about the king's challenge. On an armored steed of snowy white, St. George rode forth,' blah, blah, blah. Look." Daisy pointed to the picture of the handsome, golden-haired St. George in the next tapestry. "It looks just like him, doesn't it? The dirty stinking rat. Then he rode to the cave of the dragon. The dragon bore down upon him. Its head was immense and its tail fifty feet long.'"

Jesse broke in: "Do you think Emmy's going to get that big?"

"Yeah. No. Maybe. I guess so." Daisy buried her head in her arms. "I can't read any more, Jess. They're going to talk about smiting the dragon. I can't stand it."

It upset Jesse, too, but he read the rest of the story silently. When he'd finished, he switched off the computer.

"How bad was it?" Daisy asked, lifting her head, her face pale and her blue eyes filled with worry.

Jesse nodded. "He pierced the dragon beneath the wing with a sharp spear . . . where the dragon didn't have any scales. Then he found this humongous treasure in the dragon's cave and *Prince* George and his princess lived happily ever after in Uffington Castle."

"So are you thinking what I'm thinking, Jess?" Daisy asked.

Jesse nodded quickly. "Sadie. *Sadra*," he said.

"Uffington. *Huffington*," Daisy said.

"Princess Sadra and Sadie Huffington are the *same* person," they said together.

Before they could take their thinking any

further, Uncle Joe called up to them from the kitchen. "Dinnertime, you guys! Come and get it!"

They had skipped lunch. Up until a few minutes ago, Jesse's stomach had been growling, but now he wasn't the least bit hungry. "I don't think I can eat," he said.

"Me neither, but we've got to," Daisy said. "St. George's girlfriend has probably kidnapped the professor, and we're the only ones who can save him. We need our strength."

"We need more than that," Jesse said. "We need a *plan*."

Uncle Joe had made a pasta salad for dinner. It wasn't the cousins' favorite meal, but they shoveled it dutifully into their mouths.

Aunt Maggie, who had been in her air-conditioned advertising office all day, was cool and chipper. "You kids look a little careworn. Is something wrong?"

The cousins shook their heads.

"It's the heat," said Uncle Joe.

The cousins nodded.

"I keep telling you," said Aunt Maggie, "you should go to the town pool."

"Too crowded," said Daisy.

"No dogs allowed," said Jesse.

"Tomorrow we're taking Emmy to the Dell to

dunk her in the brook," said Daisy.

"Poor thing," Aunt Maggie said. "I wish you'd let me give her a nice, cool summer haircut."

Both cousins set down their forks with a bang and said "NO!" loudly and firmly.

Aunt Maggie laughed and shrugged. "Have it your way, but honestly, you two, she'd be much happier if you'd let me take the shears to her. The fur will grow back by winter, you know."

Daisy tried to keep her voice level as she said, "I've seen how sheared sheepdogs look, Mom. They look naked and defenseless—and—and—and—"

"Completely undignified," Jesse finished for her.

"Well," said Aunt Maggie, trying hard not to smile, "we can't have an *undignified* sheepdog running around the place, can we? And speaking of dogs, we've got ourselves a new celebrity in town."

Uncle Joe, Jesse, and Daisy all perked up and asked, "Who?"

Aunt Maggie grinned. "That gorgeous redhead who trains dogs on TV," she said. "How about that? Little old Goldmine City has bagged itself a hot celeb."

Daisy flicked a glance at Jesse. "You mean Sadie Huffington?"

Aunt Maggie nodded brightly.

Meanwhile, Jesse and Daisy were furiously banging each other's knees beneath the table.

Aunt Maggie took a long sip of iced tea, then said, "She even bought a house. A castle, in fact. Up on Old Mine Lane. You know the one, Joe? Built by the mining company during the Gold Rush. It's been vacant and walled-up for years."

"Well, what do you know?" Uncle Joe said with a wide grin. "Before they put up that big wall around it, we kids used to mess around up there. We played a game. It was called Storm the Castle."

Daisy slept fitfully that night, thinking of snake-eyed Sadie Huffington just across town from them. When she finally got out of bed and went into Jesse's room to see if he was awake, too, she saw that his bed was empty. It didn't take her long to find him in the kitchen, watching a rerun of *Top Dog* with the sound down, his nose not three inches away from the small screen.

Daisy waved her hands between Jesse and the TV. "Are you okay, Jess?"

"Sure," said Jesse, not taking his eyes off Sadie Huffington. "I'm studying her technique. Just look 'em dead in the eye and never let your steady gaze waver."

Daisy switched off the TV.

Jesse blinked. "What's the big idea? You made my steady gaze waver."

Daisy rolled her eyes. "So long as we're both awake, we might as well figure out a plan."

"Okay," Jesse said, and he followed her obediently upstairs.

It wasn't much of a plan, but like some of their successful plans in the past, it started with spying. After breakfast the next morning, they told Uncle Joe they were going up to Old Mine Lane to check out the old castle and its new owner.

"Beware the patented Ten-Yard Stare," Uncle Joe said, his voice going all eerie. Then he added, "And no trespassing on private property, remember."

"Don't worry, Poppy," said Daisy solemnly. "We're just checking it out. She won't even know we're there."

"Oh, yes, she will!" Uncle Joe said with a wink. "Remember, she's a witch."

"Right," said Jesse with a sickly smile. "We'll try to remember that."

They took Emmy's breakfast out to the garage. While she worked her way through a bag of frozen cauliflower, Jesse and Daisy briefed her. They left out the part about the dragon-smiting, but they told her everything else they had learned: about the missing professor and about Sadie Huffington's really being Princess Sadra, about her coming to Goldmine City looking for her boyfriend, St. George.

Emmy listened in stony silence and then burst out: "That dame is bad news!"

"Pretty much," said Jesse, wondering where Emmy had picked up a word like *dame*. Surely not in one of their library books.

"I bet she's got the professor under lock and key," Emmy said. "We have to find him!"

"We will," said Daisy.

"And then spring him!" said Emmy.

"First Kilimanjaro, then Everest," Jesse said, invoking one of the professor's favorite sayings, which meant "one step at a time."

Daisy said, "In this case, Kilimanjaro is Sadie Huffington's castle on the other side of town. We're going to start by spying on her . . . which means it's leash time for Emmy."

Emmy grumbled, "Why do *I* have to be the dumb dog all the time?"

"Maybe because Daisy and I can't turn into dogs?" Jesse suggested.

"But I *hate* being a dog. It *itches*!" Emmy said.

"We can always give you some of Miss Alodie's

valerian tea," Daisy said, moving to get the thermos from the backpack.

"Oh, very well!" Emmy said, and grumpy dragon masked into equally grumpy dog.

Jesse attached the leash to her purple Great Dane collar. Then the cousins wheeled their bicycles out of the garage and Jesse set out, leading the way, with Daisy and Emmy bringing up the rear. They rode right down the center of Main Street because it was deserted. Everyone was indoors with their air-conditioners, and the little town hummed with the sound of the units turned up to high.

Choosing the least steep streets, they gradually worked their way up into the foothills of Old Mother Mountain. At least that's what most of the townspeople called it. To Jesse and Daisy it was now the Hobhorn, in honor of their friend, Her Royal Lowness Queen Hap, ruler of the hobgoblins of the Hobhorn, whose kingdom lay inside the mountain.

Old Mine Lane dead-ended a quarter of a mile from what had once been the entrance to the gold mine. They knew that the old castle sat smack at the end, not that either of them had ever seen it. It had been blocked off from outsiders by a high wall overgrown with bushes and vines since before they were born. The number of houses along the road began to dwindle until there were just weed-choked vacant lots. The cousins finally arrived at the end of the road, where a brand-new plywood wall loomed at least fifteen feet high. It was the kind of wall you'd see at a city construction site, except this one didn't seem to have any peepholes for curious pedestrians to look through.

The cousins parked their bikes and waded through the weeds over to the wall. A big new sign warned, NO TRESPASSING. GUARD DOGS ON PATROL.

"Guarding the poor professor would be my bet," Daisy said.

Emmy growled, baring her teeth, the fur along her spine standing up.

"I know just how you feel, Em," said Jesse. "Let's check it out."

They walked along the wall, Emmy leading the way with her snout, nosing around for an entrance or a gate or a driveway. But they just kept following the plywood around until about fifteen minutes later, when they found themselves right back where they had started.

"Weird," the cousins said together, exchanging looks of deep perplexity. How did anyone get in or out? On the other side of the wall, they heard a loud, persistent buzzing sound.

Jesse looked around. There wasn't even a tree

nearby to climb to get a look over the wall.

"We need a ladder," said Daisy.

"Or a good leg up," Jesse said.

"Will I do?" Emmy asked, startling them both by suddenly unmasking into a dragon.

"Emmy!" Jesse and Daisy cried out together and looked around, afraid she would be seen.

"Don't worry. No one will see," Emmy said. "Come. Climb up onto my shoulders and spy."

Jesse hesitated. "It won't hurt you?" he asked.

"Do I look like a delicate dragon to you? Don't be a dork," Emmy said. "Climb." She turned around.

Jesse climbed up the ramp of her tail, his sneakers getting surprisingly good traction, and made it up as far as the back of her neck. But even if he were to stand on top of Emmy's head (which did *not* seem like a good idea), his own head would still be a good three feet from the top of the wall. He signaled to Daisy, who nodded and quickly scrambled up after him.

Jesse said to her, "I'll give you a boost up and you spy."

Jesse bent down and offered Daisy a stirrup made from his linked hands. Daisy placed her hands on his shoulders and her foot in his hands. Jesse grunted as he lifted Daisy up. She wasn't very heavy, but Jesse felt himself wobbling beneath her weight.

"I have you, Jesse," said Emmy. He felt her talons enclosing his calves, steadying him.

"I'm up!" Daisy whispered, holding on to the top of the wall and peering over. She was amazed at how new the castle looked, as if the last stone had been set into place only that morning. "Wow!"

"Ask her what she sees," Emmy whispered up to Jesse.

Jesse whispered up to Daisy, "What do you see?"

Daisy whispered back, "It looks *exactly* like the castle we saw online, Jess. It's got three stone towers, two small and one big. And the ramparts are made of wood."

"Are they riveted with sarsen stones?" Jesse asked.

"What's a sarsen stone?" Emmy whispered.

Daisy ignored them both. "I see squint holes," she said, "and killer holes, too."

"*Murder* holes," Jesse corrected.

"*Whatever*. And it's double-walled."

"Ask her what the buzzing noise is," Emmy told Jesse.

Daisy heard Emmy's question. "Lots of things. Lawn mowers. Trimmers. Other landscaping tools,"

Daisy said. "There's a whole crew of workmen cutting grass and whacking weeds on the grounds outside the wall. Jesse, it really is a life-size replica of Uffington Castle. And to think it's just been sitting here . . ."

Jesse said, "St. George built it when he was head of the mining company a hundred years ago."

"And Sadie Huffington used magic to fix it up," Daisy said. Either that, or the army of sweating, shirtless workmen who were now toiling away on the lawn had worked very hard and very fast to whip the castle back into shape. Now they were digging holes for saplings, setting the root-balls into the holes, filling in the holes, and making neat circles of stone around the newly planted trees. A harnessed team of dogs dragged a sled loaded down with piles of cut stone.

Emmy whispered up to Daisy, "Tell us more."

Just then, Sadie Huffington strode through an arch in an outer wall. Even in the heat, she wore a long black coat that reached her ankles.

"I'm looking at the Top Dog herself," Daisy said.

"Yikes," Jesse said. Daisy felt Jesse's arms begin to tremble beneath her feet.

"She's wearing a black coat that looks exactly like St. George's," Daisy reported.

"Boy! She must be boiling," said Jesse.

"I don't know . . . she looks like a pretty cool customer to me," Daisy said as she watched Sadie Huffington stop before the dog team and reach into a cloth sack slung across her shoulders. "Ugh," she said.

"What's going on?" Jesse whispered, giving Daisy's legs an impatient squeeze.

"She's got a bunch of dogs pulling a sled," said Daisy. "And she's got this bloody sack full of raw meat . . . and she's feeding the meat to the dogs."

"Hey, do you think those are the dogs that are missing from the pound?" Jesse said.

"That's exactly what they are," Daisy said. Sadie Huffington was walking among the men now. "Oh, wow! She's feeding the *men* raw meat, too!" she whispered. "*Ick.*" As each workman got his bit of bloody raw meat, he chewed it up, not neatly like a man, but sloppily and greedily like a dog. Sadie scratched one of the men behind the ear. Another man scratched his armpit, then shook himself from head to foot.

"Holy moly," said Daisy. "I think she's done worse than just stolen them from the pound."

"*What?*" Jesse and Emmy both whispered fiercely.

"The men," said Daisy. "I think Sadie might

have turned some of the *dogs* . . . into *men*."

"Whoa!" Jesse said. "Really?"

"Well, they're eating raw meat without using their hands or getting grossed out," said Daisy. "And they're panting. If they had tails, I bet they'd be wagging them."

Jesse's arms started to shake again. "Whoa again," he whispered.

"She's nothing but a witch," Emmy said. "A wicked, *wicked* witch."

Daisy watched as Sadie Huffington bent to examine one of the rock circles. She rose up and, raising her switch, thrashed the nearest worker. No red meat for him! "She just whacked one of the men with that whip of hers," she reported grimly.

"Witches make very bad Keepers," said Emmy in a loud whisper.

It saddened Daisy to see any living creature, man or dog, being treated this badly. She looked away and scanned the ramparts, nearly crying out when her gaze fell upon two of the biggest dogs she had ever seen. They were pacing the battlements just outside the large tower.

"What's the big tower called, Jess?" Daisy whispered.

"The donjon," Jesse told her.

"Right, and you said it's where they kept

prisoners in olden times?" Daisy asked.

"Yep," Jesse said. "My arms are getting tired. Are you almost done spying, Daze?"

"Just a sec," Daisy told him. She couldn't take her eyes off the dogs. Everything about them was huge: their heads, their paws, their blue-black tongues, their eyes. The one nearest Daisy stopped and turned its enormous shaggy head in her direction. Then it opened its jaws and let loose a howl that vibrated the wood beneath her fingers. Daisy reared back and lost her grip on the wall. She teetered so wildly that Jesse lost hold of her, then Emmy let go of Jesse, and all three of them went toppling toward the earth.

CHAPTER FOUR

HIGGLETY PIGGLETY POP!

"What's the big idea!" Daisy whispered furiously. She dabbed her tongue on the bottom of her shirt and showed them the dot of blood. "Look! You guys made me bite my tongue!"

Emmy, masked again into dog form, whined apologetically.

Jesse cocked a thumb toward the road. "We've got company."

The dogcatcher's truck made a slow turn in the cul-de-sac. Ms. Mindy leaned out the window and called to them, "What are you kids doing so far away from home?" She looked a lot less cheerful and considerably more frazzled than she had the morning before at the library.

"Checking out the blackberry bushes!" Daisy called back to her. "My pop knows we're here."

Ms. Mindy nodded. "Well, news flash. I've had ten reports of runaway dogs since my shift started this morning. First the break-in and now this. If I were you, I'd take my doggie on home and sit tight till we figure out what's going on."

"Sure thing!" Daisy told her.

Jesse and Daisy and Emmy watched as the truck turned around and went slowly back up the road.

When the dogcatcher was out of sight, Jesse lay back in the weeds and felt the sweat pouring off him. All around, the weeds buzzed with the sound of cicadas. It was a hot sound, like live electricity. He knew they needed to pick themselves up and figure out how to find the professor, but it was too hot to move and almost too hot to think. "I wonder if Ms. Mindy has any idea those dogs she's looking for are all on the other side of that plywood wall."

"There's no way she could know," Daisy said. "And we can't tell her, either. For all *we* know, Sadie Huffington can turn people into dogs just like she turns dogs into people."

"I wonder what kind of dog I'd be," Jesse mused.

"A mutt, probably," Daisy said.

"Good," Jesse said. "Give me a mutt any day over one of those nervous Nelly breeds."

"How can you say that?" Daisy said. "Emmy's a breed, and she's no Nelly."

Emmy woofed.

"Emmy's a *dragon,* you dork," Jesse said.

"Oh, right," Daisy said, laughing.

Jesse said, "Do you think one of those dogs could be the professor? What kind of dog would she turn him into, I wonder. She called him a hound dog, but I'm thinking he'd be one of those nifty little terriers, you know, like in *Higglety Pigglety Pop!*"

"I think he's a prisoner in the donjon," she said.

Jesse sat up quickly and looked at Daisy. Her face was bright pink from the heat and she was chewing on a long blade of grass. "What makes you so sure?" he asked.

"Just before you guys let go of me? I saw these two giant black dogs patrolling the ramparts just outside the big tower. I swear, they were the biggest, scariest dogs I've ever seen. Their tongues were dark blue and their teeth were . . . I don't even like to think of those teeth. Those vicious dogs have a job to do—and that's guarding the very important prisoner in the tower. I'm sure of it."

Jesse nodded. "They *sounded* big, like maybe Tibetan mastiffs. I wouldn't want to tangle with *one* of those, let alone two. Well, if they're guarding the professor, then we need to find a way around them."

"But how?" Daisy said. "We can't leave him there much longer! Who knows what she has planned for him."

Jesse sat there in the buzzing weeds and thought hard. "I've got it!" he said after a moment. "We go to the library and look for a book about the historic homes of Goldmine City. The castle is bound to be in it. Maybe it'll have floor plans and we can find a way to get into the tower without passing the mastiffs."

"Brilliant!" said Daisy, scrambling to her feet. "Let's go."

Emmy leaped up, too, and yipped with enthusiasm.

They retrieved their bikes and took off, the cool breeze drying their sweaty backs as they coasted downhill into town. Parking in the rack in front of the library, they climbed up the wide stone steps. Daisy knelt to fasten Emmy's leash to the Chicken Box while Jesse grabbed ahold of one of the big brass door handles and pulled. The door didn't budge. It was locked. He tried the other door. That one was locked, too. He cupped his hands to the glass and peered into the library. The lights were off. "It's closed!" he said with a groan. "In the middle of a weekday! How could they do this to us? Why?"

Daisy pointed to the handwritten note taped to the door.

Temporarily closed. Preparing for the
Pets Allowed Party. See you at six!

"Right. Forgot all about that," said Jesse.

Daisy vibrated with impatience. "Where are you, Mr. Stenson?" She turned to Jesse. "Do you think he's in the back room? I bet if we knock real hard, he'll come. I'm sure he'll let us in to get a book. He's got to. I mean, we have special privileges.

This is an emergency. How could he say no?"

With Jesse and Daisy pounding on the door and Emmy throwing herself against it, they managed to kick up quite a ruckus. But no one came. Finally, they quit banging and leaned their hot foreheads against the cool glass. Suddenly, Daisy straightened and cried out, "Jess, look! Somebody's in there. See? Over there, by the dinky water fountain?"

Next to the low water fountain, the one for the littlest kids, Jesse saw someone a good deal smaller and odder-looking than a little kid. It looked like a he, with a flimsy little torso and long, gangling arms and legs and a great big noggin—sort of like one of the house-elves in the Harry Potter books, only dustier-looking and with sharper features. Everything about his head was sharp: the bones of his skull, the big nose that hooked down and the big chin that hooked up, the jutting cheekbones, the pointy ears, and the piercing eyes that turned up at the corners—all topped off with a tuft of hair the color of dust bunnies. And this very peculiar-looking creature was, at that very moment, staring directly at them . . . and beckoning!

Emmy let out a shrill bark and the creature jumped into the air, darted across the library, and disappeared into the adult stacks.

They stood for a while, noses pressed to the

glass, hoping the funny little guy would reappear. Emmy wouldn't quit barking, so eventually the cousins gave up.

"What was it, do you think?" Daisy whispered to Jesse, her eyes round with wonder.

Emmy barked once.

"I don't know, but I think Emmy does," Jesse said. "Let's get her home quick and find out." When Jesse unfastened Emmy's leash from the Chicken Box, she practically yanked his arm out of the socket dragging him down the library stairs. It was all Jesse could do to get on his bike and fit his feet on the pedals as Emmy pulled Jesse homeward, with Daisy pumping like mad to keep up with them.

The moment they shut the garage door, Emmy unmasked into a dragon. The first breathless words out of her mouth were *"That was a shelf elf!"*

"Really?" asked Daisy.

"What's a shelf elf?" asked Jesse. "And can it help us find the professor?"

Emmy squeezed her eyes shut in thought, then opened them. "Beats me." She hung her head in shame. "Some dragon I am. I have no idea what a shelf elf is or whether he can help us find the professor."

"Well, whatever he is, I think you pretty much

scared him away with all that barking," Daisy said.

Emmy sank down onto her haunches and looked even more miserable. "I ruin everything in the end, don't I?" she said.

Daisy said, "You were excited, that's all."

"Believe me," Jesse put in. "If I were a dog, I would have barked my *head* off. That thing was *amazing*."

"He was," Daisy agreed. "And the party is to-night, so maybe we'll get a chance to see him again. *And* find the book that will help us get into the tower and rescue the professor."

"But we can't just sit around until then. We need to *do* something!" Jesse said.

"If I don't do something to cool myself down," Daisy said, "my brain's going to boil over and I'm not going to be much use to anyone, including the professor. Let's go take a dunk in the brook."

"And then we can go to the barn and visit the Museum of Magic collection," Jesse said. "Remember, Miss Alodie said that's where we should go when in doubt, which we are."

After putting their bathing suits on under their shorts and throwing together a late picnic lunch, the cousins and Emmy left for the Dell. As they had done so many times before, they walked to the rear of the backyard, crawled through the tunnel in the laurel bushes, and poked their heads out into the Dell. That was their name for the abandoned dairy barn and the pasturelands surrounding it, which were divided by a brook. Normally, Emmy would have transformed into a dragon the instant she emerged from the laurels, but today she had made a grudging promise to remain masked.

"Just in case Sadie Huffington has any spies lurking," Jesse said.

They walked along the brook until it widened into a crystalline pool beneath the branches of their favorite weeping willow, its delicate green fronds trailing in the water.

"Hey, Willow!" Jesse called up to it.

"Mind if we borrow a piece of your shade?" Daisy asked.

"We'll just be a few minutes," said Jesse. "Then we have things to do."

The weeping willow fluttered some of its long green fingers toward them, lightly brushing the cousins' faces. Since there wasn't even a whisper of a breeze that day, Jesse knew that this was the dryad spirit inside the tree welcoming them into his shade. Earlier in the summer, St. George had imprisoned the hobgoblin queen beneath the ground in this willow's root-ball. Neither willow nor hobgoblin had been very happy with the arrangement.

With his root-ball no longer weighed down by a goblin, the willow seemed positively perky now . . . for a weeping willow, at least.

Jesse and Daisy spread their towels out in its dappled shade and stripped down to their bathing suits.

Daisy was the first to wade in. Even in the deepest parts, the brook wasn't very deep. The water came up only to Daisy's chest, but Jesse knew it was as cold as the Arctic Ocean. She pinched her nose and ducked right under. It took Jesse a little longer to get wet. He liked to get used to the frigid water one toe at a time. But Emmy bombed ahead of him and then bounded out for a good long shake of her sopping wet coat . . . all over Jesse.

All three of them stayed in the freezing cold water until Daisy's lips began to turn blue, then they crawled out onto the bank to dry out and eat their lunch.

They had finished eating and Jesse and Daisy were packing up when they heard Emmy barking. She was standing on the other side of the brook, tail rigid, head raised, barking fit to bust.

The cousins gathered their things together and waded across the nearest shallow spot in the brook. Emmy turned and ran across the pasture toward the barn. By the time Jesse slid the big barn door closed behind them, Emmy was already unmasked and hunkered down over the makeshift table—old planks laid across sawhorses—that held their collection.

If you didn't know any better, you would think it was just a bunch of old junk: a farmer's ancient three-legged milking stool, some rusty old horseshoes, antique hinges, animal skulls, pressed flowers, pinecones, and a crusty old metal ball about the size of a peach. The cousins called it the Sorcerer's Sphere.

Ever since the day she had hatched, the sphere had held a powerful fascination for Emmy. She reached down and plucked it up in her talons. "I like this!" she said, as if she were discovering it for the first time.

"We know you like it, Em." Jesse yawned widely and glanced at his wristwatch. "You've *always* liked it."

"Pack this," Emmy said, tossing Jesse the sphere.

Jesse barely managed to catch it two-handed. "For the party?" he asked.

"For the party," Emmy said.

Turning the rusty ball around in his hand, Jesse

said slowly, "I don't know, Em. We've never taken this away from the Dell."

"Do what she says," Daisy said. "If this is what Emmy thinks we need, then this is what we're taking. Thanks for the tip, Em."

"Finally!" Emmy said. "Someone who really understands me."

Jesse was hurt. "I understand you, too, Em. I was just making sure this was the right thing to do."

"Trust the ladies," Emmy said, "and pack the sphere, Jesse Tiger."

Jesse put the sphere in the backpack. "I'm packing the sphere, ladies. Are you happy?"

"For a grumpy dragon," Emmy said, "I'm practically dancing with joy."

"And does the grumpy dragon promise to make nicey-nice with the other dogs at the party?" Jesse said.

"The grumpy dragon promises," said Emmy. "I will even let them sniff my butt."

When Uncle Joe dropped them off in front of the library, there were kids on the front walk holding cages and pet carriers, saying good night to their parents. Jesse had never seen any of the kids before. The kids he knew, Daisy's friends from school, either weren't coming or were still at sleepover camp. But that was okay. Since he had moved twenty-six times in his life, he was used to strangers.

Sitting in the front seat of his old truck, Uncle Joe eyed the vast amounts of stuff they had brought with them. "You guys need any help carrying?" he asked.

"No, thanks, Poppy," Daisy told him. "We're good."

Daisy grabbed the covered dish while Jesse took charge of Emmy's leash, and they each carried a sleeping bag under one arm. Jesse wriggled into the backpack, which contained, among other things, their toothbrushes, a washcloth, the Sorcerer's Sphere, and Daisy's wildflower notebook, just in case they needed to write anything down.

Daisy gave her father a peck on the cheek. "See you tomorrow. Say good night to Mom for us."

Uncle Joe reached over and mussed Jesse's brown mop of hair, which was Uncle Joe's way of hugging. "Aunt Maggie's going to ask if you packed a comb," he said.

"Of course he did," Daisy spoke for Jesse. "And maybe he'll even use it."

Jesse and Daisy went up the front walk and

climbed the stone steps to the library. Daisy drew up short in the doorway. "Pee-yew. This place smells like a gorilla's armpit," she said.

It did smell like a zoo, but Jesse kind of liked it. The library was swarming and buzzing with all manner of pets and their keyed-up owners. Jesse counted at least twenty of each.

Peering out from between Jesse's legs, Emmy began to growl ominously.

"Nicey-nice," Jesse reminded her.

Daisy tugged at Jesse's sleeve and pointed. Jesse nodded. One half of the library, the adult section, had been blocked off with orange plastic tape. That was exactly where they had last seen the shelf elf.

"We've got to try and get over there," Daisy whispered to Jesse.

"I don't think we're allowed to cross the orange tape," said Jesse.

"Would you cross the tape if it meant helping the professor?" Daisy asked.

Jesse nodded. "I guess we've got to try and get over there."

From across the room, Mr. Stenson saw them and seemed eager to take leave of the little girl with the big snake coiled around her waist. Joining them, Mr. Stenson said, "Good evening, Ms.

Emmy! Now, this is my idea of the perfect pet. We're glad you could join us."

Emmy sat up tall and dutifully offered him her right paw. "Oh, my! What manners!" said the librarian, shaking the paw. "And would Ms. Emmy care for a party hat?"

"Sure, she would," Daisy said, with hearty enthusiasm. "Wouldn't you, Em?"

Emmy whined.

"I'll let you do the honors." Mr. Stenson handed Daisy a party hat with an elastic chin strap. Daisy knelt and fit the hat carefully on Emmy's head, then stood back to admire the effect of the sparkly silver paper princess tiara. Emmy looked up at her Keepers with reproachful eyes.

"She's the belle of the ball," Mr. Stenson said.

"She is, isn't she? Um, Mr. Stenson?" Daisy was just about to ask him whether it would be all right if they checked out the card catalog on the grown-up side of the library, but Mr. Stenson was reciting the rules for them.

"We keep the dogs on leashes and the rodents, lizards, birds, and other critters in their cages. No feeding the animals people food and no teasing, prodding, poking, or otherwise provoking the animals."

"Got it," said Daisy. "Would it be okay—" she started again.

"Would you kids excuse me? I see more guests arriving," Mr. Stenson said as he breezed away, leaving Jesse and Daisy standing in the middle of the floor. They looked around. The long wooden reading tables had been shoved off to the sides, leaving a wide-open space for kids and their pets to mill around in. One of the tables held cages filled with smaller animals, like lizards and hamsters. A single goldfish flitted nervously around in a small bowl.

"I bet no one would notice if we just sneaked over there," Daisy said.

"Since we don't have our invisible pills, I think we should probably try asking first," said Jesse. He cleared his throat and said, "Hello, Mrs. Thackeray?"

Mrs. Thackeray, the weekend librarian, was wearing an oversize hot-pink T-shirt that declared her to be a Library Goddess. She was kneeling before a cat carrier and cooing at the large tabby cat staring dismally out the small mesh window. Their party hats in disarray, the canine guests were dragging their masters toward the carrier.

"Hey, kids," said Mrs. Thackeray, not taking her eyes off the cat in the carrier. "Poor kitty. She's scared witless. Can't say that I blame her. It's a dog's world here tonight."

"Mrs. Thackeray," Jesse said, "would it be all right if Daisy and I went over and looked at the grown-up card catalog? There's this book that we really, really need. . . ."

Mrs. Thackeray sat back on her heels and peered at him curiously over the rhinestone rims of her eyeglasses. "Why in the world would you want to do a thing like that, Jesse? You're here to party, you two! Or should I say, you three! Now, go play video games with the rest of the mob."

Most of the other kids were, sure enough, over in the computer lab, crowded around a single station whose *bloops, blops, blips,* and *zaps* indicated that a video tournament was underway. Jesse and Daisy dumped the backpack and their sleeping bags in the big pile along with everyone else's stuff. Jesse handed Daisy the leash.

"Okay," said Jesse. "We asked nicely, and now we have to take the law into our own hands. I'm going to try and cross the orange tape and get to the card catalog. Wish me luck."

"Good luck," Daisy said solemnly, and watched him wander off casually in the direction of the orange tape. She carried their dish over to the food table and busied herself reading the labels on some of the other dishes: CLIFFORD THE BIG RED HOT DOG CHILI; WILBUR THE PIGS IN BLANKETS; BUNNICULA'S

CARROT COCKTAIL NIBLETS; LASSIE COME HOME FRIES. Daisy printed a label for their dish, HIGGLETY PIGGLETY CARAMEL CORN POPS, and set it down between CHOCOLATE CRICKETS IN TIMES SQUARE and BALTO'S MALTED MILK BALL SOUFFLÉ. Emmy began to whine and roll her eyes. Daisy turned around, expecting to see some dog with its nose in her butt.

Instead she saw six dogs crouched in a shy half circle, staring at Emmy, heads all cocked to the same side. They looked nothing if not bewildered. Daisy wondered whether the dogs sensed deep down that Emmy was not really one of them.

"My dog's a registered purebred," boasted Dewey Forbes, the poodle's owner. Daisy had known Dewey since kindergarten.

"Emmy's purebred, too," Daisy said, straightening the paper tiara.

"Yeah? Well, since when do purebred sheepdogs have *forked* tongues?" Dewey asked.

Emmy pulled in her tongue and shut her mouth with a snap. Sheepdogs didn't have emerald-green eyes, either, but apparently that detail had escaped Dewey's attention. People tended to notice the forked tongue, so Daisy always had an explanation ready. "She tried to lick a frozen water pump one winter morning and it split the tip of her tongue in half," Daisy said to Dewey.

Jesse joined them. "Have *you* ever tried to lick a frozen pump, Dewey?" he asked. "You should try it sometime."

"Should not," Dewey countered. "Because that would be dumb. Your dog must not be very smart."

An offended little growl escaped Emmy.

"Poodles are the smartest breed going," Dewey said. "Watch this." He held up two fingers, and the big poodle stood at attention. "Sit, Loretta."

Loretta the poodle sat.

"Down, Loretta."

Loretta crouched on the floor.

"Roll over, Loretta."

Loretta rolled over.

Dewey folded his arms across his chest and gave them a smug, satisfied look. "So?"

"So?" Jesse said.

Daisy looked unimpressed. Emmy opened her mouth, forked tongue and all, and yawned widely.

"So? I bet your stupid fork-tongued sheepdog can't do that," Dewey said.

"Why would she even *want* to?" Jesse said. "Those are boring tricks. Emmy can do *interesting* tricks, can't you, Emmy? Emmy, go fetch the backpack."

Emmy went over to the big pile of backpacks

and found theirs right away. She picked it up in her mouth by the strap and trotted back to Jesse, setting it at his feet.

"Good girl!" Daisy said, giving Dewey an I-told-you-so look.

"Open the backpack now, Emmy," Jesse said.

A crowd of kids and pets had gathered around to watch the performance. Emmy held the bag down with her forepaws while she took the small tab between her teeth and unzipped the top of the backpack.

The crowd let out an "Ooooooh!" of approval.

Jesse held up a hand to show they were not finished yet. "Okay, Emmy, now find the doggie book," he said.

Emmy poked her nose inside the backpack and pulled out *Higglety Pigglety Pop! or There Must Be More to Life*.

"Thanks, Em. Now show us how you can read the doggie book . . . all by yourself." Jesse looked around at the crowd. "She can read. She really can. She taught herself."

Emmy set the book on the floor. Then, nosing it open to the first page, she began to bark in a rhythm that sounded remarkably like the opening paragraph of Maurice Sendak's famous book.

While the kids, pets, and the two librarians

stood around and listened, Daisy moved closer to Jesse and spoke to him out of the corner of her mouth. "So. Did you break through to the other side?"

Jesse shook his head and said, "That girl with the snake cornered me. I think she was hoping I'd be scared, but I told her I used to own an African rock python twice as long when we lived in Africa. She let me hold him. He's pretty nice. His name is Slick. You should check him out."

"No, thanks," Daisy said. "The only thing I want to check out is the book on the historic homes of Goldmine City."

"At the rate we're going, we're going to have to wait until everyone's asleep later tonight," said Jesse.

Just then, the crowd in the library burst into loud applause.

Daisy looked around. "What's going on? Why is everyone clapping?" she asked.

"They're clapping because our dog knows how to read," Jesse said.

Daisy shook her head slowly and sighed. "If they only knew what other tricks she can do!"

CHAPTER FIVE

DRAGON HEAVEN

Emmy lifted her head from the book with a look of becoming modesty. But the look she shot Jesse said something more like *When can we get out of here and spring the professor from that dame's dungeon?*

"That was great, girl!" Jesse said, kneeling and

burying his nose in Emmy's fur, which still bore the faintest scent of hot chili peppers.

Daisy whispered, "Don't you think you got a little carried away?"

Jesse spoke through clenched teeth. *"Nobody calls our dog dumb and gets away with it."*

Mr. Stenson clapped his hands loudly. "Okay, kids. Now, did everybody follow the rules and feed your pets their dinner before you came tonight?"

"I fed mine crickets," a boy said.

"I fed mine a live rat," the little girl with the python said.

"I fed mine mealworms!" someone else said.

"Okay, okay, kids, thanks for sharing," said Mr. Stenson, holding up his hands. "I'm glad your pets all have full tummies, because we humans are about to fill ours, and no *begging* pets are allowed in this library tonight."

Mrs. Thackeray, the Library Goddess, dealt out paper plates, napkins, and plastic utensils as everybody lined up and filed past the food table, piling their plates high with the various pet-inspired dishes.

They had finished eating and had stuffed their dirty plates into the big plastic garbage bag when Mr. Stenson directed them to arrange their sleeping bags in a circle on the floor. Jesse and Daisy took care to situate themselves on the outermost edge of the circle, closest to the adult section. Mr. Stenson and Mrs. Thackeray had placed their sleeping bags in the middle of the circle next to a large electric lantern that Mr. Stenson had enthusiastically designated as their campfire.

After they had all lined up to brush their teeth and wash their faces in the library lavatory, it was story time. Mr. Stenson invited them, one by one, to come into the center of the circle and read aloud a few pages from the story they had chosen.

Jesse sat cross-legged on top of his sleeping bag and held the Sendak book to his chest, waiting for his turn to read. Jesse might be shy, but he was a much better public reader than Daisy. For some reason not even she understood, Daisy's voice just disappeared when she had to read aloud. Emmy burrowed into Daisy's sleeping bag and turned around with her nose poking out the top. Daisy wrapped her arms around Emmy and used her as a pillow. Megan Lowe, a prim fifth grader, opened her book and began to read aloud about a cat that had traveled with the pilgrims on the *Mayflower*.

The girl's droning voice quickly made Daisy as drowsy as a feaster with a belly full of turkey. She wondered whether the professor was allowed to eat anything in the tower. Was Sadie Huffington feeding him bread and water, or raw meat?

Then Kevin O'Hanlon, who had brought a fence lizard, read the opening chapter of *Farewell, My Lunchbag,* featuring lizard sleuth Chet Gecko. Daisy kept falling asleep and snapping awake. Were those big black dogs naturally vicious, or had Sadie Huffington bewitched them into being that way?

Next came the girl who had brought the lone goldfish. Daisy knew her only as the soon-to-be third grader who was always organizing games of wild horses on the playground. Her parents, Tina explained, had given her the goldfish, when what she really wanted was a horse. She tossed her long mane of hair and read aloud from *Black Beauty,* a deeply sad passage that Daisy only half heard.

Daisy kept her eyes open just long enough to find out what Dewey Forbes had brought to read. It was *Poodles for Pinheads,* and if you didn't happen to own a poodle, it was a real snooze.

She hoped Jesse would forgive her for missing his reading of *Higglety Pigglety Pop!,* because she really couldn't keep her eyes open another second.

Jesse's eyes snapped open. Someone had just poked him with something sharp, in the small of the back. He lifted his head and looked behind him, but no one was there. Everyone was curled up, fast asleep, wrapped in the folds of their sleeping bags. The lights were out, the air-conditioner rumbled, and the full moon shone in the big front windows of the library, washing the spines of all the books in a pale, silvery light.

He sat up and reached over to shake Daisy awake, and she popped up. She blinked and rubbed her eyes, then automatically ran the fingers of one hand through her bedhead hair while she tapped Emmy on the shoulder. The sheepdog lifted her head and shook herself awake, rattling the gold locket on her collar.

Daisy put her finger to her lips. "Shhhhh." She pointed to the other side of the library. Jesse pointed to the backpack. Daisy nodded and grabbed it.

Easing themselves out of their sleeping bags, they tiptoed away from the circle of sleepers and ducked under the orange tape. Finally, they made it onto the altogether less-familiar side of the library, where the grown-up books were. The grown-ups' card catalog computer, which Jesse had been eyeing all night long, sat on a small table near the librarian's desk. They approached it.

Jesse groped around for the computer switch. The screen lit up and the computer made a whirring sound, followed by a loud *voop*. He shot an anxious look over at the children's side. But all he heard was snoring, a guinea pig rustling in its wood shavings, and a hamster jogging in its squeaky wheel.

Jesse wiggled his fingers and keyed the words "Goldmine City Historic Houses" into the search box. The next minute, a single title popped up on the screen: *The Grand Historic Homes of Goldmine City.*

With her hands resting on Jesse's shoulders, Daisy leaned toward the monitor and scanned the description along with him. Jesse tapped the screen. There was a listing for the Presidential Palace, built in 1901 by someone named Skinner, who was the head of the Pacific Mountains Mining Company. The address was listed simply as Old Mine Lane. Daisy pulled her wildflower notebook out of the backpack, tore a corner from a page, and copied down the book's call number. Then she stuffed the notebook into her backpack and slung it over her shoulders.

Emmy led the way toward the stacks. She seemed to know her way around, which was a good thing, because Jesse and Daisy felt like strangers where the shelves were higher and the books were thicker and darker and altogether more serious-looking.

The cousins followed Emmy into the aisle marked NONFICTION. Emmy went halfway down and halted, turning to face the shelves on the left-hand side. She looked up and wagged. Jesse and Daisy followed her gaze up to where it rested on the fourth shelf.

Jesse started on the left and scanned the call numbers. In the exact spot where the book should have been was a wide gap. Jesse rose up on his tip-toes to see if the book had gotten pushed to the back of the shelf.

Jesse gasped as a head popped out and a voice said "boo!" right in his face.

It was the shelf elf!

Reeling backward, and forgetting all about his library voice, Jesse let out a startled yelp. Daisy clamped her hands around Emmy's jaw to keep her from doing the same.

The elf stuck his head out even farther and, with a long finger pressed to his lips, said, "Shhhhh!"

Daisy whispered furiously, "Shh yourself! Who are you, anyway?"

The shelf elf popped back into the gap and disappeared.

Emmy scrambled around to the next aisle over, with Jesse and Daisy right on her tail. But there was no shelf elf to be found.

"Psssst!"

They spun around. The elf was standing at the head of the aisle, hands on his hips. Then he leaped into the air and sped away.

"After him!" Jesse cried in a fierce whisper.

They took off in hot pursuit, their stocking feet skidding to a slippery halt as the elf hopped up on top of a reading table, slid the length of it, hurtled over the backs of three chairs, bounced on the seat of a fourth, and dived headlong into the fiction section. Emmy, Jesse, and Daisy ran around the table, giving chase to the shelf elf up one aisle and down another. But the nimble little man always managed to stay at least half an aisle ahead of them. Finally, at the end of the *R* to *Z* aisle of the nonfiction section, the shelf elf stopped and spun around to face them, backed into a corner at last.

"Got you now!" Jesse whispered, and he started to close in on the shelf elf.

Just as they were almost upon him, the elf shot up into the air and dived into a small hole in the floor by Jesse's feet.

"Whoa!" said Daisy.

"How did he do that?" Jesse asked.

The cousins and Emmy leaned over the small hole, then stared at each other in disbelief: How could that small elf have fit into this even smaller hole?

Daisy got down on her hands and knees and peered into the hole, trying to see where the elf had gone.

"I don't see anything," she whispered.

As Jesse watched, something started moving inside the pack on Daisy's back. A second later, it rolled out the top.

"The Sorcerer's Sphere!" Jesse cried, lunging to catch it.

"Get it!" Daisy said as the sphere bumped off her shoulder, rolled down her arm, and disappeared into the hole with a hollow *pop*.

All three of them shrank back, shielding their eyes from the blinding white light that suddenly poured out of the hole and flooded the entire library. The next minute, the stone floor beneath them gave way, like an elevator in free fall, taking them down with it. Faster and faster they fell, the cool air whistling past their ears. They screamed, then squeezed their eyes shut, rolled themselves up into tiny little balls, and prayed for a gentle landing.

A minute or two later, they alit at the bottom like feathers, upright and flat on their feet. Giddy with relief, Jesse opened his eyes. The first thing he saw was Emmy, in dragon form, with the silver paper princess tiara slipped over onto the side of her head. An even funnier sight was Daisy. Her long blond hair was standing straight up in the air. When he reached over to touch it, it crackled and sent a zing of static electricity up his arm.

"Sorry," said Daisy. "Yours looks pretty funny, too. Look at that." She pointed.

Standing before them, on a tall pedestal that resembled an oversize golf tee made of gold, was the Sorcerer's Sphere, but it was no longer a rusty sphere. It was now a beautiful, sparkling, multi-faceted ruby.

"Wow. What is this place?" Jesse said, looking around.

It had the airy indoor-outdoor feel of an enormous sports stadium or a cathedral. The ceiling—if there was one—was obscured by a blanket of thick golden fog. It smelled as sweet and rich as the air in his mother's favorite spice shop in Bangalore, India.

"It's a library," Daisy said, turning in a slow circle. "But it's not the Goldmine City Public Library."

It was a library on a gargantuan scale. They slowly set out down its broad central aisle, which was nearly as wide as Goldmine City's Main Street. They stopped here and there to peer down the side aisles. The aisles stretched out to eternity, lined with bookshelves rising to dizzying heights and jam-packed with books as massive as the one stolen from Miss Alodie's parlor—and some of them a good deal bigger. The massive tomes were bound in a rainbow of leather hues so dazzling, Jesse wanted to run his fingers along them like the keys of some fantastic piano.

Daisy rummaged in the backpack, then wrestled her hair into a bun and skewered it with a pencil. "Well," she said, when she had managed the feat, "at least now we know where that big red book came from."

Jesse wasn't looking at the books just then. He was looking at all the creatures scuttling overhead. They slid from shelf to shelf on a webwork of fine silken filaments, like mountaineers rappelling down a rock face. Jesse heard a droning noise. He recognized it as the sound of talking and muttering and humming.

"Shelf elves!" Emmy said. "What did I tell you two!"

"Right again, Emmy," Jesse said.

One of the elves broke away and began to hurtle downward at an alarming rate, landing before them with a crunching sound and a breathless little "Oof!" and a bow. And seemingly to himself: "Watch the knees now. My word!"

Jesse somehow knew instantly that this was the

same shelf elf who had led them on the wild chase through the stacks.

The shelf elf said, "Willum Wink, Chief Steward of the Shelf Elves of the Scriptorium! How may I be of service to you three today? (Or is it tonight? It's always a little hard to tell in here.)"

Something about the shelf elf's voice made Jesse want to giggle. It was high-pitched and it warbled, the way it sounds when you inhale helium from a birthday balloon.

"I, um, ah," said Daisy, and Jesse could tell by the redness of her face that she was fighting the same fit of giggles he was.

Jesse swallowed his mirth. "We're looking for a book," he said, feeling that this was the right thing to say, since it was the truth, or had been up until a few moments ago. Clearly they weren't going to find the book on historical homes here, but it might be where the big red book had come from and, just possibly, where it had been returned. Since the professor and the book had gone missing at approximately the same time, maybe there was a connection. Finding one might help to find the other.

"A book, you say? How novel! (Toss in a little shelf elf humor now and then, I always say, don't I? I do!)" Willum Wink snorted mirthfully to himself.

"Well, you've come to the right place! Do you happen to have the D-D-D-S-N?"

"The *what*?" Daisy asked.

Wink narrowed his eyes in a thoroughly suspicious squint. "Who are you *really*? And who sent you here? The Dragon Domain Designation System Number. What else? (What else, indeed!)"

Emmy piped up with a long string of babble that might have been a number, for all the cousins knew. It seemed to make complete sense to Willum Wink, who stroked his sharp hook of a chin and said, "Yes. No. Sorry. Do pardon me. That volume is in our collection, but she is currently unavailable."

"Unavailable?" Jesse asked. "What do you mean?"

The elf's upturned eyes flashed. "I mean *out*! As in not here at the moment. As in not currently on the shelf. (How many ways must I put it to make them comprehend? My sweet elfin *word*!)"

Jesse was beginning to see that the elf had a habit of talking to himself in the middle of talking to them and that whenever he did it, his eyes crossed, as if they were chatting with each other over the bridge of his nose.

"It's out. We get it," Daisy said. "But what I don't get is how can a book be a she or a he?"

The elf gave his dusty little tuft of hair a tug. "A

book can be a she or a he depending upon whether it is a female or a male," Mr. Wink said. "And this particular *she* checked herself out, let me see now (it's here somewhere, I know. Isn't it? Well, of course it is!) . . ." He opened a small notebook and hummed to himself as he flipped through the pages. He stopped and tapped a page with a finger that had twice as many joints as any human finger and a pointy nail. "Two terrestrial great moons ago."

"Two months ago, you mean? Checked *herself* out?" Jesse said.

"Yes, dearie. That's what books do here," Mr. Wink said absently as he tucked the notebook away inside his jacket and began dusting himself off with a tiny whisk broom. His jacket was brown checked and cinched at the waist with a tool belt filled with strange implements. The jacket had elbow patches, which was a good thing because the shelf elf had very sharp elbows. He tucked the little broom into a loop on his tool belt and went on: "Here, they are free to check themselves in and out as they please. They are *living matter*! Not dead, as are all the books they keep *up there*!" He pointed toward the fog above, by which the children took him to mean the Goldmine City Library.

Jesse didn't like to think of all the books he had read as being dead, but he didn't want to argue the point now. "This is a big dark red book we're talking about," he said, "with a metal ring on the cover like a door knocker?"

"Distinctive, isn't she? She has a superb sense of style, that one. Such flair! (Unlike *some* I could name, isn't that the truth? It is!) I know exactly to whom you refer. Her name is Leandra of Tourmaline," said the elf. "Leandra is one of our finest volumes."

"Leandra?" Emmy whispered faintly. "My mother!"

Jesse and Daisy stared at each other in wonder.

Emmy said to them, "Yes, that's my mother's name. I know it like my own. And to think that she was there all the time and I never knew it!"

"Ah!" said the elf. "(Now it all makes sense, doesn't it? It does!) You must be the hatchling she was so eager to meet! But I don't understand. If she's your mother, why isn't she with you?"

"Emmy's with her Keepers!" Jesse put in quickly. "That's us. We take care of her."

"You are my Keepers and I love you," Emmy said in a tremulous voice. Then she opened her mouth and wailed, "But I WANT MY MOTHER!"

"Uh-oh!" Willum Wink took a few wary steps backward.

The next moment, Emmy exploded in a howling,

bellowing gale of tears and dragon snot. Daisy dug around frantically in the backpack as Emmy flung herself down and wept and ranted and raged, flailing at the stone floor with all four limbs and her tail. Daisy finally found the blue washcloth they had packed. Reaching an arm out, Emmy snagged the washcloth and soaked it with fresh torrents.

How are we ever going to get her to stop? Jesse shut his eyes because he hated to see Emmy cry, and also because he needed to think. But before he could summon his thoughts, he felt something splatter his face and hair. At first he thought it was Emmy's tears. Then he realized it was coming from somewhere overhead. He opened his eyes, looked up, and saw that the fog was now spangled with shimmering flakes of gold that were drifting gently down onto his face and shoulders. He brushed at them.

Daisy noticed them, too, and began to brush them out of her hair and off her shoulders.

"No need to worry. (Why does everybody carry on in this fashion? My word!)" said the shelf elf. "It's just dragon dust."

The cousins stopped fussing. "Dragon dust?" they chimed.

The shelf elf looked around. "(Are we in an echo chamber? I see we must be!) Most of the volumes here are coated with the stuff. We don't even try to keep up with it. (Although we get enough grief for it, don't we? We do!) We just let it build up, and every now and then some sweet young thing like this comes along and starts carrying on and brings it all raining down. It's perfectly harmless, I assure you, and generally dissolves seconds after contact. Observe." Wink held out one long arm to demonstrate.

The cousins watched as the flakes disappeared into the fabric of his jacket and didn't even leave spots. Emmy, tears suddenly forgotten, sat up and cast the sodden facecloth aside. Opening her mouth wide, she caught some dragon dust on the tip of her forked pink tongue.

"Mmm . . . yummy. Tastes like The Time Before," she said, smacking her lips and opening her mouth for more.

Taking advantage of Emmy's distraction, Jesse turned to the shelf elf. "So you're saying that the red book is called Leandra. And that Leandra is actually Emmy's mother?"

"And that Emmy has a *book* for a mother," Daisy added, just to be sure.

The shelf elf sighed. "(My word! They just don't seem to hear it the first time, do they? They really don't!) Emmy has a *dragon* for a mother," Mr. Wink explained waspishly. "These books you see on the shelves all around you? They were all, every single one of them, full-fledged dragons at one time. When—after many centuries of life in their various domains—dragons die of natural causes or, as is unfortunately sometimes the case, are slain, smote, or otherwise terminated in an untimely fashion, this is where they come to roost."

"So," Daisy said slowly, looking around as if seeing the books on the shelves in a new light, "it's like dragon heaven."

"Think of it as heaven, with visiting privileges. Traveling privileges as well. (Come to think of it, isn't that the truth? It is!) These volumes contain the sum total of the lives of the dragons that lived them: their thoughts, ideas, sermons, lectures, homilies, theories, spells, poetry, philosophy, psychology, recipes, helpful hints, pithy sayings, games, activities, plans, hopes, fears, and dreams for those who follow." Willum Wink sucked in a deep breath, exhaled, and then smiled.

"Now *that's* what I call interesting!" said Jesse.

"Not necessarily! Oh, no! You'd be surprised what crashing bores some of them can be. But the majority really are quite worth the parchment they are printed on. Young dragons, like this one here"—the elf gestured to Emmy—"come to learn the wisdom of the ages: Tales of The Time Before, if you will. Or, alternatively, volumes from our collection can go forth and visit themselves upon dragons out in the field. Leandra joined our collection over one hundred of your years ago, after George Skinner smote her and drank her blood."

Jesse looked to see if Emmy had heard that, but the young dragon seemed to be otherwise engaged. He nudged Daisy and she nodded, smiling. Emmy was lathering herself with dragon dust. Not only was she not crying anymore, she was practically dancing for joy.

Willum Wink went on: "I'm truly sorry Leandra isn't here. (I'm actually rather concerned, now that I think of it—where could that dear girl be? I cannot imagine!) You would have loved reading her story. It was a towering saga of good versus evil fraught with emotional resonance." He fished a big, yellowed hanky out of his breast pocket and dabbed at the tilted corners of his eyes. Then he blew his hooked nose into it and stuffed the hanky away. "But it's not as if we have a shortage of books here. Oh, no! I'll have you know that we are a fully accredited institution."

Jesse and Daisy both nodded, duly impressed.

"Oh, I have it!" The shelf elf kicked up his heels and laughed merrily. "I just thought of the perfect book for you. (Oh, how I love, love, *love* matching readers with books! All the rest is just paperwork—face it, Winkie!)"

Willum Wink gathered in a silken lasso from his tool belt and tossed it high into the foggy reaches. The line went taut and then the elf began hauling something down, arm over arm. Soon a huge stack of parchment bound on the long side sailed down from on high and settled on the floor in front of them with a deep, musty-smelling sigh.

It was very big, even for this collection, but it wasn't much to look at. Unlike all the other books, this one had no colorful leather cover, and its pages were stained and ragged and torn.

"What happened to its cover?" Jesse wanted to know.

"I know. It's rather a pitiful sight, isn't it? (But never judge a book by its cover or lack thereof, I always say, don't I? I do!) We've offered to tidy him up and even give him a dashing one hundred percent synthetic cover to replace the one he's lost, but no, he prefers to bare himself in all his battle-scarred splendor. I'm sure he'll be more than eager to recount in colorful detail how he got this way. (He never misses a chance, does he? He doesn't!)" Willum Wink tapped his toe, cleared his throat, and called out: "Balthazaar? Yoo-hoo! Balthazaar of Belvedere, come forth. Eager readers await you!"

CHAPTER SIX

BALTHAZAAR'S STORY

The stack of pages ruffled sluggishly, then went still again.

The shelf elf squinted hard. "Really?" he said. "You say you are not in the mood for storytelling? Even for the Dragon Keepers of Emerald of

Leandra and the hatchling herself?"

Jesse and Daisy watched as a cloud of dark gray mist bubbled out of the parchment and formed itself into an enormous ghostly black dragon. A deep voice rumbled forth from the mouth of the giant apparition: "The long and short of it was, I was duped." In his ghostly face, his eyes, dark red as garnets, seethed with indignation.

"Do start at the beginning, please. (They'll skip ahead to the climax, if you don't watch them, won't they? They will!)" The shelf elf leaned against a bookcase, his long arms seeming to have lost all their bones as he flung them casually around his neck like the ends of a scarf.

"Very well," said Balthazaar. "Mine is the story of George Skinner and his lady, although I use the term loosely."

Jesse and Daisy settled themselves cross-legged on the floor of the Scriptorium, ready to listen.

"So is this the *true* story of St. George the Dragon Slayer?" Daisy asked. "We read one version of it already on the Internet."

"Not *my* version, you didn't!" The red eyes gleamed like a pair of reflectors caught in headlights. "What you read is *their* story: a pack of baldfaced lies. My story is the truth. In my story, George is no hero on a white steed. He is not even a knight.

And in this hallowed place, we don't even mention the words 'saint' and 'George' in the same breath."

"Then if he wasn't—excuse me, please, just this one time—*St. George*," Jesse asked, "then who was he?"

"He started out in life as George Skinner, the tanner's boy, scraping the rotting flesh from the skins of carcasses. No matter how many riches he accumulated, he never lost the stench of the tanning vat. It is the smell of death."

Daisy, remembering St. George's breath, thought she knew the smell all too well.

"And who was I?" asked the dragon. "I was a sorcerer."

"Wait a minute. You mean a *human* sorcerer?" Jesse asked.

Daisy nodded, the same question on her mind as she imagined a robed figure with a conical cap and a magic wand.

Balthazaar spat contemptuously. "I was a *real* sorcerer. Those clowns in the peaked hats were mere *students* of dragon sorcerers. But of all the powerful dragon sorcerers in all the domains, none was more powerful than I. People journeyed from far and wide to consult with me, and my rates were always reasonable and fair. I had been practicing for hundreds of years and had amassed sufficient wealth to buy the petty kingdom of Uffington a thousand times over.

"That was my first mistake, to hoard my treasure in plain sight when I should have hidden it . . . but what are riches for if not to flaunt?"

"What was the second mistake you made?" Daisy asked.

"Taking on George Skinner as my apprentice."

"St. George, er, I mean George Skinner, was your *apprentice?*" Jesse asked.

The dragon shot Jesse a look designed to discourage further needless interruption. "That's what I just said, boy. And a promising one he was, hungry for knowledge. My fatal blunder was not seeing his hunger for what it was. He was a comely lad, too, and he had turned the head of the king's daughter, the flame-tressed one."

"Princess Sadra," Daisy said.

"Princess of *Darkness,*" the dragon intoned gloomily.

Emmy broke in. "That means she's a witch!" The dragon dust shower had tapered off, and she now listened to the story while turning every which way, trying to reach an itch on her back. "Didn't I tell you two that she was a witch?"

"Yes, you did," said Daisy. She sprang up and tried to scratch Emmy's itch for her. But the dragon's squirming made it impossible. Daisy finally threw up her hands and returned to her listening spot.

"Go on with the story, Balthazaar," Emmy said. "Don't mind me."

"Don't worry. I won't," the big dragon said snappishly. "Now, where was I?"

"Sadra the witch had just become George's girlfriend," Emmy said cheerfully.

"Ah, yes!" said Balthazaar. "At first, I couldn't believe my good fortune. George was the most diligent apprentice I could have asked for. And Sadra was every bit as helpful. She even took charge of the meals. I was flattered, having a princess in charge of my scullery, but I have always had a weakness for flattery. One night, we sat together in the dining hall, as we did every night, to sup. But on this night, one taste of her wild boar stew sent me into a stupor."

"Sadra drugged you!" Jesse said and turned to Daisy. "Do you think that's how she keeps the dogs and dog-men in her power? By feeding them drugged meat?"

"That's *exactly* what she does," said Daisy. "I'm sure of it!"

"When I came to my senses," said Balthazaar sadly, "over a year had passed. My treasure trove was gone! Skinner and Sadra had made off with every last coin."

"Skinner stole *me*," Emmy said, now scratching her back against the edge of one of the bookcases, "when I was just a hatchling, didn't he, Jesse and Daisy? But my Keepers got me back."

"Would that my Keeper had been there to save me, but I had outlived my own Dear One by several hundred years by that time. I went to Uffington Castle to beg the king to intervene on my behalf. The king had always been my friend. But my friend was gone. George and his own daughter had driven him off, and now they held the castle and the kingdom. I stood outside the walls and begged them to give me back my gold. That was when they started spreading those vile rumors about me."

"You mean about you killing all the cattle and sheep?" Daisy asked.

"Yes. Maidens, too. Orphans, mostly, so there were no families to stand up for them. George made a great show of offering up those sacrificial maidens. At sunset on the night of the full moon, he would bind them to a stake outside the castle walls on a place called Dragon Hill. I would come at night and set the poor terrified creatures free. They fled and took sanctuary in the next kingdom. But their disappearance worked to George's advantage. He told the people I had eaten the maidens, and he left a pile of bones outside my home. It wasn't long before he had turned my neighbors and even my dragon associates against me."

"Hey, no fair!" Jesse cried.

"One night," Balthazaar went on, "the townspeople came for me bearing torches and clubs. The world believes that dragons are fierce, but by nature, we're not. What is more, my powers had been weakened by that long period of morbid slumber. I found I could neither flame nor fly. The mob easily overpowered me and removed my last ounce of strength by binding me in iron chains. Iron weakens dragons, you know."

"We know," said Daisy, summoning a grim memory of St. George trapping Emmy in a coil of iron chains. If the hobgoblin queen hadn't come to the rescue, St. George would have smote Emmy with the queen's own Golden Pickax.

Balthazaar continued with his story. "Once I was in chains, George came at me with a sharpened lance and pierced me through the heart."

"Beneath the wing, where you have no scales," Daisy added grimly.

Balthazaar nodded thoughtfully. "Had I known what he would do to me afterward, I might have fought harder. I suppose I should have known better. Once a tanner, always a tanner."

"Oh, no!" Daisy clapped a hand over her mouth.

"Oh, yes!" said Balthazaar. "George Skinner . . . *skinned me*: I, Balthazaar of Belvedere."

Daisy was glad that Emmy was too caught up in scratching her itch to pay much attention to the tale's grisly turn.

"He took the best and most powerful part of me for a trophy: my beautiful black scales, my magic, my essence, my soul, my identity, my pride, my *dragon skin!*" Balthazaar finished on a note that trembled with passion.

There was a moment of silence as they all mourned this inestimable loss.

In a lighter tone, Balthazaar added, "For all I know, the blackguard has it mounted on a wall somewhere."

"No," said Jesse, shaking his head. "That's not what he did with your skin, Balthazaar."

Daisy shot Jesse a curious look. "So what did he do with it?"

"You know, Daze. Think about it. What is George always wearing, no matter how hot it gets? And what has Sadie Huffington been wearing nearly every time we've seen her?"

Daisy's eyes widened. "A long black coat!" she

said, then clapped her hand over her mouth.

"Exactly," said Jesse, "a long black coat . . . *made from dragon skin!*"

Daisy dropped her hand and said, "We'll get your skin back for you, Balthazaar, won't we, Jess?"

Jesse stared at her as if she had just sprouted a second head, and sputtered, "We will?"

"Of course we will," she said. "At least the half on Sadie's back. I mean, we have to rescue the professor anyway. We might as well get the coat while we're at it."

"*If* we can rescue the professor," Jesse said, his jaw tight. "Have you forgotten the team of Tibetan mastiffs guarding the tower? *The biggest dogs you've ever seen?*"

"We'll just stick to the plan," Daisy said confidently. "We'll get the book about Goldmine City houses and find a way to sneak around those big black dogs. Right?"

Balthazaar, who had cocked his transparent head toward their conversation, spoke up. "Castle, you say?" he rumbled. "What castle would this be?"

"The replica of Uffington Castle that St. George—er, George Skinner—built a long time ago in our hometown of Goldmine City," Jesse explained.

"A replica, you say? Hmmm," said Balthazaar

thoughtfully, scratching the crown of his head with a sicklelike talon. "Well, if it is indeed an exact copy, I will gladly show you the plans, especially if it will get me back even one half of my beloved long-lost skin."

He reached down and flipped through the pile of parchment at his feet, laying the book wide open before them and smoothing the pages out lovingly. "Gather round, my younglings," he said.

The book was so big, Jesse and Daisy had to scramble up onto the bottom edge to see what was on the page. In faded black ink was an elegant set of drawings detailing the floor plans of Uffington Castle.

"How come these are in your book?" Jesse asked.

"Because I was the castle's architect. The king of Uffington held a contest, and naturally," he said with a modest shrug, "my plan won."

Daisy whipped out the wildflower notebook, pulled the pencil out of her bun, and began copying the floor plans onto a fresh page.

While Daisy did that, Jesse spoke to her in an undertone. "I'd hate to raise Balthazaar's hopes only to dash them. What if we can't get the coat back? I mean, for all we know, Sadie Huffington is even more powerful than St. George. She seems so to me, at least. Doesn't she seem that way to you, Daze? I mean—"

Daisy cut short his fretting with a tug on his arm. "Look here, Jess." She showed him the plans she had copied into the notebook and pointed. "See? There's a secret passage that goes underground, tunneling beneath the outer walls and coming up inside the castle. See? It comes out here, in the throne room. Once we're in the throne room, we go over here, to the gallery. See this set of twisty stairs? It leads up to the main tower, which is where the keep or the donjon is."

"Which is where we think the professor is being held prisoner!" Jesse said, forgetting his worries. "Brilliant!"

"Exactly. Totally bypassing the giant dogs!" Daisy beamed at him.

They hopped off the book and launched into the happy little prospector's dance to celebrate their perfect plan.

"It's all very well for you to frolic," Balthazaar grumbled, "but if I were you, I shouldn't leave my friend very long in the clutches of that evil woman."

Jesse and Daisy froze.

"You're right," Daisy said. "We've got no business dancing while the professor is her prisoner." Then she looked up into the ghostly face of the dragon storyteller. "Thank you for the plans, Mr. Balthazaar. We promise to do our best."

"Cross our hearts," Jesse said.

"Never mind your hearts. Just use your brains. You'll need all your lobes to outsmart that wily wench," said the dragon, his garnet eyes now on fire with hope. Then he dissolved into a black vapor that bubbled back into the pages of the book and disappeared.

"What did I tell you?" the shelf elf said with pride.

"You're right, Mr. Wink," Daisy told him. "That was an *extraordinary* book. Thanks for recommending it. But now we have to go. We have lots to do."

"Where's Emmy?" Jesse asked.

Mr. Wink pointed. Emmy stood behind a bookshelf, holding a long pole that had a hook on the end of it. Whatever it was, it made for a perfect back-scratcher. The expression on Emmy's face was one of pure bliss.

"I guess she finally reached that itch," Jesse said, smiling.

"Come on, Emmy," Daisy said. "Let's go."

"Must you scratch and run? (Why are they always in such a hurry these days? Who knows!)" Willum Wink's shoulders sagged in disappointment. "I was *so* hoping you'd stay long enough to view the Scriptorium's Special Collection."

"You have a collection, too?" Jesse said.

"We'll come back and see it another time," Daisy said.

"Why not now?" Jesse said.

"Ah!" said the elf with a grin. "I know a connoisseur of collections when I see one. Step this way."

Daisy held Jesse back. "What are you doing?" she whispered furiously.

"I'm going to see the collection," Jesse said. "And so are you, Daze. Remember what Miss Alodie said? She said 'Look to the collections.' I bet that's what she meant. Not just our own collection, but the Scriptorium's, too."

Daisy's eyes grew wide. "Jess, you're a genius!"

Jesse blushed.

They followed Willum Wink down the wide main aisle until they entered a different sort of space, fit out with long, low stone tables, upon which elves swarmed over countless books spread out in various states of disrepair.

"We call this the Recovery Laboratory," Willum Wink said.

Some of the elves they passed wore blue jackets. Others wore red jackets.

"What are they doing?" Daisy asked.

"Those are bibliotechnicians in blue," the elf explained. "Bibliotherapists in red. Specialists. (And stuck-up ones, too, aren't they? My word, they are, indeed!) They do what needs to be done to keep all our volumes in good repair. They refresh faded inks, mend torn pages, sew raveling bindings, tidy the headbands and the foot bands, glue down peeling endpapers."

"What do the bibliotherapists do?" Jesse asked.

Mr. Wink halted. "You know, I've always wondered that myself. It's all very sensitive and hands-on and intuitive, but it's strictly hush-hush. Ah, here we are!"

They came to a place where the worktables had given way to row upon row of enormous display cases, their glass fronts sparkling in the foggy golden light.

Emmy, who had left the pole behind, ran ahead and began to work her back against the edge of one of the cases.

"Emmy!" Daisy scolded, afraid she would smudge the glass.

"That's quite all right!" said Willum Wink. "The young ones have so little self-control. But she'll do no real harm."

Jesse signaled to Daisy and she joined him by one of the cases. On display were skulls of animals she recognized along with skulls of animals she was pretty sure didn't exist in their world. There were fangs and bones and precious stones and strange-looking pressed leaves and equally strange flowers. One entire case held an arrangement of cracked geodes and the names, presumably, of the famous dragons that had hatched from them: Timor of Quartzite, Mina of Feldspar, Saffron of Hematite. Their names alone made Daisy want to hear their stories.

"We need some cases like this for our Museum of Magic," Emmy said.

Jesse and Daisy turned to look at the dragon.

"That would be cool, wouldn't it?" said Jesse.

"Super-ultra-fantastic-cool," said Emmy as she continued to scratch. She was so good-natured that Daisy found it hard to worry about the persistent itch of hers.

Jesse had moved on to the next case. "You guys," he called out to Daisy and Emmy. "This stuff is *awesome*!"

Daisy and Emmy joined him. In the case were weapons and shields with crests emblazoned on them. There were helmets and coronets molded to a full-grown dragon's head. In the next case were dragon-size broaches and rings and necklaces studded with a dazzling assortment of gems. In yet another were household items: bowls and goblets and cutlery and a massive mortar and pestle made of jade. A relatively smaller object, flat and made of silver, with an intricate design of a dragon on the top, drew Daisy's attention.

"I wonder what this is," she said.

"Maybe it contains some anti-itching powder for me," Emmy said.

Jesse and Daisy both turned to her again.

The dragon was grinning widely, her emerald eyes gleaming with mirth. Was their junkyard dog making a joke? Her first in twelve days! The cousins chuckled appreciatively.

Then Daisy turned back to the case and tapped it. "Mr. Wink, what's this thing here?" she asked the elf, who had been standing by with quiet pride as they pored over the exhibit.

"That would be . . ." He took out a monocle and fitted it into his right eye, peering into the case. He snapped his fingers, trying to summon the name, murmuring, "(What do they call them, now? You know! I do?) Ah, yes. A Toilet Glass."

Jesse and Emmy both burst out laughing.

"A Toilet Glass," said Jesse.

"Do you make wee-wee in it?" Emmy asked.

Willum Wink leveled at Emmy the now-familiar Squint of Disapproval. "Your humor, young lady, escapes me."

Daisy explained. "It's just that where we come from, toilets are what we call the place where we go, where we make, um . . ." She groped for a more delicate way to say it.

Wink raised both hands, warding off further attempts to explain. "Say no more!" he said, removing his monocle. "I glean your meaning. A garderobe! (How odd they are, these Keepers and their kept one!)" He explained, "This is not an object of the garderobe. (Is it? My word! Goodness, no!) It is an object of the boudoir, a lady's private chambers."

The three of them continued to look puzzled, so the shelf elf said, "(The depth of their ignorance is unfathomable, is it not? It is!) Permit me." He fished a set of keys from a loop on his belt, unlocked the case, and opened it. Removing the object from the display, he held it in one hand and popped open the top, revealing a disk of metal on the inside of the lid. Wink polished it with his hanky and then shone it at them.

"It's a mirror!" said Jesse.

"Right you are," said the elf.

On the bottom of the disk was an empty well that Daisy figured was probably for face powder or blush. "I think it might be a lady's compact!" she said, taking it gently from the elf's hands. "It's really beautiful!" She held it up and looked at her face in the mirror. She was amazed at how good she looked, considering everything she had been through. Even her hair now looked smooth and shiny and straight. Why, she looked . . . like a beautiful princess!

Mr. Wink was saying, "It's quite a remarkable piece. It belonged to Princess Sadra during the height of her reign at Uffington with George Skinner. He'll always be George Skinner, the tanner's boy, in Balthazaar's book and in every book that sits upon our shelves, I might add. (But I digress, don't I? I do!)

"*Anyway*, Sadra prized her vanity set. She had the finest silversmith in the kingdom of Uffington fashion it to her exact specifications."

Daisy said suddenly, "Could we have this . . . Toilet Glass?"

Willum Wink gave her the Squint, then snatched the glass back and said, "Never! It is the express property of the Scriptorium. (Face it, Winkie, you never should have opened this case in the first place. You have no one to blame but yourself, do you? Guilty as charged!)"

"But wouldn't Sadra be happy to get it back?

You said yourself that she had loved it," Daisy said in her best wheedling voice.

"Of *course* she would be thrilled to have it back!" Wink said. "But since when has the happiness of that crimson-haired *harridan* been a goal of ours? (My word! Keepers these days! Do they know *anything*? I am certain they do not!)"

"But we might be able to use it," said Daisy.

Jesse's face lit up as it dawned on him where she was going with the idea. "We can trade it for the coat and get Balthazaar his skin back," he said.

"And maybe get the professor back in the bargain," Daisy whispered to Jesse. Then she said to Willum Wink, "Surely Balthazaar's skin is more valuable to the Scriptorium than one measly piece of . . . silver."

"Pretty-please with sprinkles on top?" Emmy joined in.

Willum Wink pursed his lips, tugged at his hair with both hands, and went completely cross-eyed for a full minute as he held a silent conference with himself. At the end of it, he uncrossed his eyes and placed the Toilet Glass in Daisy's hands. "Take it," he said, "and use it wisely. (These Keepers are smarter than they look, aren't they? They are!)"

"Thank you!" said Emmy and Jesse together.

"And we will use it wisely," said Daisy.

"So how do we get back to Goldmine City?" Jesse asked.

"Simple!" said the elf. "You just have to fly up there"—he pointed skyward—"and drop the sphere into the hole. It's a bit tricky, but nothing you can't manage. The sphere is your pass to and from the Scriptorium. Drop the sphere into the hole in the center of the dome and . . . Bob's your uncle!"

Daisy grinned. Jesse's dad's name was Robert, and she always loved it when people used that expression . . . because Bob really *was* her uncle. Then her grin faded. "How are we supposed to fly up to the top of the dome? I hope we don't have to climb up there with one of your flimsy little ropes, because I'm telling you right now, I flunked ropes in gym."

"My word, no," said Mr. Wink. "The Scriptorium ropes would never lend themselves to such rigorous gymnastics."

"Then how do we get up there?" Jesse asked. "Fly?"

"Hmmm," said the elf, at a loss for suggestions.

"We don't exactly have wings," Daisy said.

"Oh, yes we do!" said Emmy.

CHAPTER SEVEN

THE FLEDGLING

Jesse and Daisy whipped around to find their dragon beaming at them. "Guess what?" she said.

"What?" the cousins said.

"This is what!" She raised her arms, and with a soft *pop-pop*, a pair of gossamer wings unfurled on

either side of her body. They weren't a bird's sort of wings, made up of feathers. They were most emphatically a dragon's sort: made up of a vast, delicate web of struts and frets forming patterns that looked more like the work of some ingenious imagination—an elaborate Japanese parasol, perhaps, or the sails of some magical airship—than something born of nature. Jesse couldn't take his eyes off them.

Willum Wink looked mortified. "How old did you say your dragon was?"

"We didn't," said Jesse. "But she's eight weeks, three days, and"—he looked at his wristwatch and counted silently—"fourteen hours." He grinned happily.

Mr. Wink sagged against one of the display cases and clapped a hand over his chest. "Forgive me. I am quite taken aback. I've heard of this happening, but I have never seen it with my own eyes. My blessed elfin *word*! A premature fledgling!" he shrieked.

"What's a premature fledgling?" Daisy asked.

After the elf had managed to compose himself, he said, "A premature fledgling gets its wings many years before the developmentally predictable time. Normally, dragons are at least fifty years of age before they even begin to cut their wings. How this happened . . ." He paused and then raised a finger as one theory occurred to him. "Just *possibly,* it might have had *something* to do with the ingestion of the *dragon dust.*"

"Wow," said Jesse. "I might have eaten a flake or two myself. Does that mean I'm going to sprout wings, too?"

Willum Wink folded his arms across his chest and gave Jesse the Squint.

"Throw them a little Dragon Keeper humor now and then, I always say, don't I? I do!" Jesse said, crossing his eyes.

"Pretty good." Daisy laughed, then said, "Okay, guys, let's go get that sphere."

Emmy and Wink led the way back through the workroom toward the stacks, carrying on an animated conversation just out of the cousins' earshot. Daisy and Jesse walked behind them with their eyes on Emmy's wings. Even partially furled, they were an impressive sight.

Daisy squeezed Jesse's shoulder. "We're going to fly on Emerald's back!" she whispered. "Isn't this excellent?"

Jesse felt nowhere near as gung-ho as his cousin. "Do you think we'll be all right? It's not like she's had flying lessons or anything," he whispered back.

"She'll be fine!" Daisy assured him, giving his shoulder a sporty little shove. "It's dragon magic, Jess, relax."

Jesse nodded, but he felt uneasy. Heights scared him. His parents always kept a basket in the Jeep for when they drove up steep mountain passes. Jesse put the basket over his head so he wouldn't have to look down. He wondered if Willum Wink had any baskets handy in the Scriptorium.

They came upon the ruby sphere, exactly where they had left it, glowing on its big golden golf tee. Jesse reached up and took it. The ruby felt much smoother in his hand than the rusty old sphere had. He stared into its crystalline depths for a moment before slipping it into the side zipper pouch of their backpack.

Daisy took the bag from him. "Let me do this," she said.

Jesse cleared his throat uneasily. "So how is this going to work? I mean, what are we supposed to hold on to? Do we get safety belts or harnesses or anything like that?" he asked, only half joking.

"Take out my dog leash, please," Emmy directed Jesse.

Jesse rummaged around in the backpack and found the leash. "Got it," he said, pulling it out.

"Hitch it to my collar," Emmy said, bowing low to make it easier for Jesse.

"Now unbuckle my collar and run the loop end of the leash through the collar," Emmy said.

"I get it!" Jesse said with a surge of relief. "It's like a rein. I hope it holds," he added nervously.

"Jesse Tiger," said Emmy with a fond shake of her head, "don't be afraid. I'm giving you a rein, but only because it will make you feel safe. You really won't need it. No matter what happens, you two will stick to my back like goo."

Jesse laughed in spite of himself. Emmy was more grown-up now, but she still chose the wrong word now and then. He was glad she did. It reminded him of the early days, when she was a baby. "Like *glue,* you mean . . . because of dragon magic?"

Emmy nodded. "My scales will hold you. That is the way of it. Don't you see? You have kept me safe since the day I hatched, and now it is *my* turn to keep *you* safe . . . on my back while I fly through the air!"

Jesse nodded and smiled. "Thanks, Emmy," he said.

"You're welcome, Jesse. Let's go find my mother!"

"Hold it, Em. Before we do that we have to find

the professor and spring him from Sadie Huffington's prison," Daisy said.

Emmy nodded eagerly. "First spring Professor Andersson and second track down Leandra of Tourmaline. We have busy times ahead, don't we, Dragon Keepers!"

Jesse and Daisy smiled at her. They were both so happy to have the old good-humored Emmy back with them again. Jesse was pretty sure that the grumpiness and the premature fledging were connected. Perhaps getting wings really *was* like cutting teeth.

Emmy flattened herself so Jesse and Daisy could climb up onto her back from her tail without crushing her wings. In spite of the wings' vast expanse, there was something fragile about them. There was just enough room between her wings for them to sit and hold the looped leash.

"Just a minute!" said Daisy. She quickly took the pack off her back and swung it around to the front.

"Good thinking," Jesse told her. "I guess we're all set, then."

"I know we are!" said Daisy with a huge grin on her face. "Good-bye, Mr. Wink. Thanks for everything. It was great meeting you."

"Yeah, I hope we see you again sometime," Jesse said. "Wish us luck."

"Good luck, and I assure you, the pleasure was all mine. It's not every day one witnesses a premature fledging. That's one for the books! (When they get wind of this, they'll be *vermillion* with envy, won't they? Raging royal purple, they'll be!) Well, this isn't getting it done, is it?" He pulled a long telescopelike instrument from his tool belt and peered through it into the aisle ahead. Then he tucked it away. "Are you ready, Emerald of Leandra, for your maiden flight?"

Emmy nodded. "All ready, Wee Willie Winkie. See you in the stacks!" Emmy said and rose up onto her hind legs.

Jesse and Daisy leaned back, gripped the leash, and braced themselves. On either side of them, Emmy's wings extended outward, almost touching the stacks on either side. Emmy began to run, taking long, low, springy steps forward, faster and faster, until she sprang up and—just like that!— they were airborne! Jesse felt his stomach flip. *Dragon magic,* he kept telling himself. He even risked removing one hand from the leash to wave at Willum Wink, who waved back at them from far below.

"Holy moly!" said Daisy. She dropped the leash and lifted both hands over her head like a rider on a roller coaster. "Emmy's right, Jess. We're stuck here. We don't even need to hold on to the leash."

Jesse believed her, but he didn't feel it in his bones, so he kept one hand on the leash.

Two or three pumps of Emmy's wings sent them surging upward toward the layer of yellow fog. Below them, the Scriptorium lay like a small city. The aisles stretched out beneath them like roads, and the stacks, swarming with shelf elves, were like skyscrapers. Then, suddenly, it all disappeared as they pierced the bank of yellow fog and just as quickly broke through it into the clear air above.

Emmy's ascent abruptly became vertical. Up and up she rocketed, the wind whistling past Jesse's head. His ears popped. And then Emmy stopped.

"Why is she stopping?" Jesse whispered to Daisy in a panic. Daisy shook her head and grinned, as if she couldn't wait to find out what was going to happen next.

Emmy shifted, nose pointed downward, and plunged! Jesse nearly swallowed his tongue. Daisy squealed with delight. The next instant, Emmy whipped around and they were flying *upside down!* Jesse felt the blood rush to his head. He gripped the leash with both hands, squeezed his eyes shut, and felt the sting of Daisy's hair whipping him in the face.

"Whoa!" Daisy hollered.

Up they went again, Daisy laughing so hard, she was crying and sputtering. It felt like torture to Jesse. He couldn't wait for it to be over. And then, just as Emmy halted on the next dreaded invisible precipice preparing for one of those spine-jarring nosedives, Jesse heard Emmy whisper to him, sounding exactly the way she had on that first day up on High Peak, from inside the thunder egg: *"Jesse Tiger!"* she said now. He opened his eyes. *"Let go!"* she whispered. *"Just let go."*

And, just like that, he did. He relaxed his tense muscles and his clenched jaw and even released his death grip on the leash, and before he knew it, it was as if he were flying along with Emmy. Not that he had sprouted wings. It was just that something *inside him* had opened up, much like Emmy's beautiful purple-green wings. And along with the opening up came a ticklish sensation that swooped from the crown of his head to the pit of his stomach. It wasn't the kind of ticklish that made you want to yell "Stop!" It was the kind of ticklish that you gave in to and, once you did, wished would never, ever stop.

But it did stop, or at least it slowed down, as the golden ribs of the great dome rose into view above them and Emmy pumped her wings toward the small, dark hole at the top. Then her wings collapsed suddenly as something—some powerful force coming from the hole—began to pull them toward it, like smoke up a flue.

"Get ready to pitch the sphere!" Jesse shouted over the mounting noise pouring out of the hole like water from a powerful faucet.

Daisy nodded, unzipped the side pouch of the backpack, and took out the ruby sphere. After she offered it to Jesse for a good-luck kiss, and kissed it once herself, Daisy took aim and tossed it up toward the hole.

The sphere hovered in the air, about a foot below the opening.

Oh, boy! Jesse thought. *What happens if it misses and falls to the ground? Will we have to fly back down and search the miles of stacks for it?*

Jesse's worries came to an abrupt end when, with a loud *pop!*, the hole sucked the sphere upward. Then, one by one, they each followed. Jesse watched as Daisy, hair first, got sucked into the hole. When Jesse's turn came, he felt like toothpaste in reverse: getting squeezed *back* into the tube. He was vaguely aware of Daisy's sneaker smashing into his face and Emmy's delicate head beneath his own feet as, with supersonic speed, they all hurtled, screaming, toward the blinding white light.

Finally, they found themselves in a heap on the

floor in the corner, at the very end of the *R* to *Z* aisle, in the adult nonfiction section of the Gold-mine City Public Library. Jesse and Daisy were clutching Emmy's leash, which was still attached to Emmy's purple Great Dane–sized dog collar, which was still around the neck of Emmy the sheepdog, who looked as if she had just gone through the full cycle of an automatic car wash . . . without a car. Oddly enough, the cardboard tiara, still on her head, looked good as new. But the sphere, which lay on the floor near Daisy's left foot, was its rusty old self again. Daisy picked it up, dropped it into the backpack, and zipped it closed.

The small hole through which they had been pulled into the Scriptorium and then sucked back was now neatly sealed closed with a silver plate that looked like a miniature manhole cover. An *elf hole* cover!

The three slightly addled adventurers picked themselves up off the floor and reeled back toward the children's side. The moon still shone in the front windows, only now it had risen much higher in the sky. The place still smelled like a zoo. The same hamster was still jogging in the same squeaky wheel and the same guinea pig was still stirring in its bed of shavings.

They fell into their sleeping bags, Jesse into his

and Daisy and Emmy into Daisy's, too exhausted to even zip themselves in. All three fell into a deep and dreamless sleep.

As soon as Daisy opened her eyes, she had a feeling that she was the last one to wake up. She looked around the library. All the other kids had already rolled up their sleeping bags and now sat in a circle on the floor eating breakfast. Daisy rolled over and dozed off again.

The next time she opened her eyes, she saw the blue washcloth. Hadn't she left it behind in the Scriptorium? She reached for it. It was neatly folded and smelled clean and yet deliciously spicy, like the Scriptorium. She smiled, imagining Mr. Wink leaning over a washtub full of soapsuds with his sleeves rolled up to his very sharp elbows. She turned her head the other way and saw Jesse sitting on his rolled-up sleeping bag, reading and eating.

"Is that a sandwich?" Daisy croaked, her voice hoarse from all the screaming she had done while flying on Emmy's back. *Flying on Emmy's back!* She hugged herself with happiness.

"It's a Green Eggs and Hamwich," Jesse said. He had her wildflower notebook open in his lap, and she could tell he was studying the plans she had copied down from Balthazaar's book the night before. She looked around for Emmy and saw her crouched nearby, eyeing Jesse's breakfast and licking her chops.

"Hey," Daisy said. "How come you guys didn't wake me up?" She sat up and stretched.

"You looked really exhausted," Jesse said. "Your hair, especially," he added with a snicker.

Daisy reached up and felt the large rat's nest up there. She got to her feet and rolled up her sleeping bag. Then she trudged off to the washroom and used a comb to work the tangles out. It took a long time. When she was finished, her hair stood up around her head like a lopsided lamp shade. So much for the beautiful princess she had seen in the Toilet Glass.

Daisy went into the big room and swiped the last two Green Eggs and Hamwiches off the tray. Then she wandered casually off into the back room, where she tossed one of the Hamwiches to Emmy. Emmy swallowed it whole. It wasn't until the sheepdog was licking her chops and begging for another that Daisy realized Emmy had eaten her first meat without spitting it out.

"I gotta tell Jess!" she said.

But when she and Emmy went back into the big room, Mr. Stenson and Mrs. Thackeray were bundling paper plates into garbage bags and clapping their hands to remind everyone to pack up all their stuff.

"We wouldn't want you to leave anything valuable behind . . . like a gerbil turd or a rabbit pellet," Mr. Stenson said with a tired smile.

Grown-ups had begun to show up, parents of the younger kids and those who lived too far away to walk home. Mr. Stenson and Mrs. Thackeray flung open the front doors and cheerfully said goodbye to the kids, their pets, and their parents. It looked to Daisy as if the librarians couldn't wait to air the place out and return it to its normal booksmelling, *No* Pets Allowed state.

As soon as she stepped outside, Daisy felt a burst of cool, fresh air on her face. "Emmy's got her wings, we've got the castle plans, and the heat wave's over!" she crowed.

Emmy barked joyfully.

"Yay!" Jesse joined in.

On the way home, Daisy told Jesse about Emmy eating her first meat for breakfast.

Jesse nodded thoughtfully and said, "So maybe now that she has wings, her eating habits will change. I wonder if anything else will change."

Daisy wasn't sure how she felt about that.

When they had closed the garage door and Emmy had unmasked, the first question out of

Emmy's mouth was "Is there any of your mother's pot roast in the refrigerator?"

Daisy hesitated, then said, "I don't think so, but there's a package of minimally processed sliced turkey."

"Bring it on," Emmy said eagerly. "I'll *gobble* it right up."

Jesse pointed at Emmy and burst out laughing. "Gobble! That's a good one, Em. Did you hear that, Daze? Emmy made *another* joke!"

But Daisy was too unsettled by the new carnivorous Emmy to find anything funny. She couldn't help but think that the next step in Emmy's evolutionary development was the hunting and eating of small, defenseless woodland creatures.

When they went into the house, they saw a "welcome home" note on the kitchen table from Aunt Maggie, who had already left for work. They looked around for Uncle Joe and found him in the upstairs hallway switching off the attic exhaust fan.

"It'll be nice to give this poor overworked sucker a rest," he said. He turned and gave Daisy a long, curious look. "Did you do something new to your hair?"

Jesse snorted.

"I like it," Uncle Joe said, cocking his head to one side. "It's light and . . . poufy."

"I slept on it funny," Daisy muttered. Then they followed Uncle Joe from room to room as he switched off the other fans and they told him all about the party. He chuckled over *Poodles for Pinheads* and then asked, "Where are you three gallivanting off to today?"

"After I take a shower and wash my *poufy* hair, we're going back up to Old Mine Lane," Daisy told him.

Uncle Joe grinned. "That's some place, eh? But I'm not sure how Ms. Huffington will feel about you playing Storm the Castle with her brand-new old home."

"Don't worry. She's too busy bossing the landscapers around to even notice us," Daisy said.

"I bet she's showing them who's Top Dog," Uncle Joe said.

The cousins showered and changed clothes and then went down to the kitchen to make lunch, including the entire package of sliced turkey for Emmy. Then they packed Miss Alodie's tin of Knock-'em, Sock-'em Dog Biscuits, the nearly full thermos of valerian tea, their weird earmuffs, the Toilet Glass, and, most important of all, Daisy's wildflower notebook with the floor plans of the castle inside it.

After that, they made a quick detour to the Dell to drop off the sphere at the Museum of Magic. While they were disappointed that it was back to being a rust-encrusted sphere, it had certainly proven itself to be even more magical than either of them had ever imagined. On the way to get their bikes, they passed the Rock Shop. Uncle Joe called out to them through the screen, "Have fun storming the castle!"

"We will!" they shouted back as they hopped on their bikes and headed off. This time, Daisy led the way and Jesse rode behind holding onto Emmy's leash. They took care riding through town—which was much more lively now that the heat had broken—then rode up into the foothills of the Hobhorn and down to the dead end of Old Mine Lane. They stashed their bikes in some overgrown lilac bushes there near the turnabout and waded through the weeds toward the wall.

"Okay. What's the plan?" Daisy said.

Jesse took out the wildflower notebook, opened to the plans, and passed it to Daisy. "We find the secret passageway, rescue the professor, and then . . ." He trailed off.

"Sounds like Storming the Castle to me," said Daisy.

"More like a *stealth* storm," Jesse said.

Daisy, studying the plans, tried hard to remember the precise position of the towers behind the plywood walls. She turned slowly and stopped, facing the side of the mountain. "If the towers are lined up the way they were back in the kingdom of Uffington, the outside entrance to the secret passageway should be right about *there,*" she said, pointing to a wall of sheer rock in the side of the hill.

The three of them walked over to the hillside. There they found a neat square hole cut into the rock.

"If I didn't know better," Jesse said, "I'd swear that was a little doggie door."

Daisy nodded. "No way we're going to fit through it."

"So it's probably not the secret passageway," Jesse said.

Emmy lifted her head and barked twice, which meant *you've got that right.*

Daisy was greatly relieved. She hated the idea of crawling into a dark hole, the way they had done the day they had discovered the door in the earth near the barn.

"Okay, now what?" Jesse said.

"Any ideas, Emmy?" Daisy asked.

Perhaps because it wasn't a question that had a one-bark or two-bark answer, Emmy unmasked. Daisy stole a quick look around to make sure they were alone.

Emmy said, "Maybe when the Slayer had this place built, he changed the location of the entrance to the secret passage."

"Okay," said Jesse, "so we circle the plywood fence until we find it."

"Plan!" said Daisy. "And if someone comes, Emmy, mask quickly."

"Quick as a lightning bolt!" Emmy assured her.

Three abreast and spaced widely apart, they proceeded to move in a slow circle around the plywood fence. They came upon an old unicycle with a flat tire, a crumpled shopping cart, an ancient icebox, the long front seat of an old pickup truck with the stuffing oozing out, some rusted wire bedsprings, and three busted umbrellas. Eventually, they arrived back where they had started.

That was when Emmy shouted, "Bingo!"

The cousins joined her. She was standing about ten yards away from the sheer rock face, next to a moss-covered statue of a skinny dog facing the castle.

"It's a whippet!" said Jesse.

"What's a whippet?" asked Daisy.

"It's a superskinny dog once bred for hunting. And look," he said, clearing away the moss. "It's got jeweled eyes."

"Wow! Are those real emeralds?" Daisy asked.

"Peridots," said Emmy, peering closely at them. "Trifling stones . . . compared to emeralds."

Jesse muttered under his breath.

"What did you say?" Daisy asked him.

"I said, 'yellowish green, like a snake.'" He shivered gloomily. "This is the entrance to the secret passageway, all right."

Daisy scraped away the moss from the dog's face and neck. Its slender neck appeared to be jointed. She grasped the head in both hands and tried to move it.

"Let me," said Emmy. She held the head in one hand and turned it easily, like unscrewing the cap on a bottle. The dog's sharp muzzle now pointed toward the cliff face.

Daisy said to Emmy, "Try pressing the eyeballs."

Emmy poked her talons into the dog's eyeballs. Sure enough, the eyeballs could be pressed inward and a section of the cliff face before the three opened up, like a set of sliding stone doors.

CHAPTER EIGHT

A COLD SPELL

Jesse got that sudden sinking feeling in his chest.

Daisy boldly approached the doorway. Jesse hesitated, then went along with her. Through the wide doorway, a set of marble steps wound off to the right and disappeared into the pitch-dark.

Daisy pounded her forehead and groaned. "We forgot the flashlight!"

"Not a problem!" said Emmy. She knelt and gathered a few rocks from the ground, rubbing them briskly in her hands.

"What are you doing, Em?" Jesse asked.

"I'm making light of things," she said, chuckling. She opened her hands. The stones gave off a bright glow.

"Holy moly," said Daisy.

"Better than a flashlight," said Emmy, "and no batteries required." She handed Jesse a stone. He was afraid it might be hot, but it was as cool as . . . stone. Emmy handed a stone to Daisy and kept a much larger one for herself.

"All set, then," said Jesse. He remained rooted to the spot, waiting for someone else to make the first move.

"I'm the one with claustrophobia, so you go first," Daisy said, nudging him forward.

"Right," he said, and stepped up to the opening. It was like entering a sort of foyer, with the walls and ceiling all made of the same smooth golden marble as the stairs. The tawny stone sparkled in the light from his hand. It didn't *feel* like an underground space. It wasn't like the old mine, all made of packed dirt. This was more like an underground palace, spanking clean. Why, then, did it make him feel so uneasy? He put on a bold front. "Daze, I don't think you're going to mind this a bit," he told her.

Daisy went behind him, with Emmy at her heels. "Not bad," she said, looking around. "Beats the heck out of tree roots and earthworms." When she spoke, her breath came out in puffs of steam, the way it does on a wintry day.

"Yeah, but somebody forgot to turn on the furnace. It's freezing in here," said Jesse.

Daisy gave him a superior look. "It's just a secret passageway, Jess," she said. "We're not moving in."

"Right," Jesse said shortly. "In that case, let's get going." He tramped down the steps as they curved away in the direction of the castle. "So far, so good." But the deeper they went, the colder it got. Jesse's nose started to run and his fingertips grew numb.

"Not good," Emmy said from behind him. "The Scriptorium was much nicer. It smelled good. This place smells . . . like a doo-doo factory. This place is bad."

"I'm with you there," said Daisy, rubbing her arms for warmth.

Jesse took a whiff. They were right. The air smelled gassy. "It reminds me of a catacomb!" he said, forcing some enthusiasm into his voice.

"Catacombs are cool. They're basically underground graveyards. I've been to catacombs in Rome and Mexico. They've got cubby holes in the walls crammed with old bones and mummified remains."

"That's all we'd need!" Daisy said sarcastically. "Let's just get on with storming the castle, okay?"

"Okay," said Jesse. "I was only trying to have a little fun."

"We're not here for fun," said Daisy, a deep frown creasing her brow. "We're here on Dragon Keeper business."

"Dragon Keepers can have fun," Jesse said under his breath. *What's with Daisy?* Except for the time she was coming down with chicken pox, he had never seen her act so grumpy. It made him grumpy just to be around her. He continued down the winding stairs, his sneakers soundless on the smooth stone steps, until he came to the bottom. The narrow hallway ahead extended a few yards and then ended at a stone wall, with passageways branching off to the right and left.

"Looks like we've run into a T intersection here." Jesse stopped and turned to Daisy and Emmy. "Right or left?" he asked.

"Impossible." Daisy went alongside him and held her glowing stone over the notebook. "See for yourself," she said. "There's no T here."

Jesse said, "Well, I'm looking at a *T* in this passageway. Are you sure you copied the plans down right? You were in a rush."

Daisy scowled. "Of course I copied them down right!"

"Well, I'm only saying . . . ," Jesse said, moving the stone of light first one way, then the other.

"And *I'm* only saying," said Daisy, narrowing her eyes, "that I copied down exactly what was in Balthazaar's notebook, and the underground passage went in a straight line to the castle. No *T*."

Jesse folded his arms across his chest. *What's her problem?* It's not like she was cutting wings. "Fine!" he told her. "But that doesn't help us figure out which way to go, now, does it?"

"Why are you looking at *me*? Why do I always have to be the one to make the decisions?" she said.

"Maybe because *you're* the one who gets all grumpy unless it's you making the decisions," Jesse said. "Listen to yourself! You are being *so* grumpy right now. Isn't she being a grump, Emmy?"

Emmy turned her head away to avoid taking sides.

"A grump?" Daisy said. "At least I'm not a worrywart like some people I could name!"

"Grump."

"Worrywart."

"Bossy."

"Wimp."

"Meanie."

"Wuss."

Emmy stepped between them. "No name-calling. Remember, sticks and stones can break your bones, but worms can never hurt you."

Jesse was so steamed, he didn't even bother to correct her.

Emmy added softly, "Keepers, we are in this stinky secret passageway and we need to find out which way to go to get into the castle. So please stop being rude to each other and think. Remember what Balthazaar said. We need to use our brains. Both lobes. Or, in my case, all five."

Daisy threw up her hands in disgust. "You're so smart, why don't *you* decide, *Dragon Brain*?"

Jesse stared at Daisy in astonishment. It was one thing to be rude to him. But there was no excuse for being rude to Emmy. It didn't, however, seem to bother Emmy in the least.

"Okay!" she said graciously. "Let's see: Jesse's toe is pointed right, so I say we go right."

"Thank you, Emmy," Jesse said with exaggerated politeness as he led the way down the passageway to the right. Something came into view up ahead. At first he thought a woman was standing in their path, but then he saw it was a pillar with a woman's head carved into it. It was so creepy! The details in her face were strikingly lifelike—and somehow familiar, as he moved closer. The expression on her face was unnerving. Her eyes and mouth were wide open in a terrified scream. Farther down the pillar, two hands emerged from the stone. The longer he stared, the more he thought the face looked exactly like the nosy woman's who lived across the street.

"Hey, Daze, doesn't she look like Mrs. Nosy-Britches?" Jesse asked.

Daisy flicked it a glance as she passed by. "Not really," she said.

Jesse walked on, but froze on the balls of his feet when a blood-chilling scream echoed along the passageway at his back.

"Help, police! It's a dragon! A real, live dragon, I tell you! After it!"

Jesse swung around and looked at Daisy and Emmy.

Daisy was clutching her elbows and her teeth were chattering in her head. "W-w-why are we stopping? *Again*?"

"Didn't you . . . ?" Jesse started to say.

"Didn't I *what*?" Daisy asked snappishly.

Her nose was running and her lips were nearly

blue, but it was obvious to Jesse that she hadn't heard the scream. Nor had Emmy. Both of them stared at him expectantly, impatient for him to move on. Only Jesse had heard the scream. He turned around and faced front. *Or had he?* He stuck a pinky first in one ear and then the other and whirled it around vigorously. "I'm really starting to *hate* it down here."

"And I suppose you think I love it?" he heard Daisy mutter testily under her breath. He didn't like her tone, but he didn't want to start again, so he said nothing more.

They rounded another bend and all three of them stopped and sagged in dismay against the stone wall.

"You're kidding!" said Daisy.

"Give me a break," Jesse said.

They held their glowing stones up high to see better. Before them lay a vast chamber, filled with what looked like an acre of short walls forming different shapes—slight curves and hard *L*'s and *U*'s and *S*'s and looping curlicues—set at odd angles, forming passageways.

"I know what this is," Jesse said slowly. "It's a maze." Even in activity books, with a pencil in his fist, Jesse didn't like mazes.

Daisy blew the hair out of her eyes. "I suppose

you're going to tell me that this isn't in the plans, either?"

Jesse shook his head slowly. "Nope," he said. "Okay, Emmy, which way now?"

Emmy looked around the maze. "Let's see . . . I like . . . *that* way . . . over by that wall, there," she said, waving a talon in the direction of a short curved wall that was covered with a colorful mural.

Jesse nodded and led them all past the curved wall. After seeing (and hearing) the scary screaming woman (who may or may not have been Mrs. Nosy-Britches), Jesse didn't want to look too closely at anything else in that place. Nevertheless, he felt his eyes being pulled toward the mural.

It showed a scene that looked familiar. He realized with a start that it was a painting of the small village in Tanzania where his parents were. Here was the hut where his parents lived, and there was the long, low tin roof of the clinic. And there was the bush in the background. He turned away quickly and shook his head. *That can't be.* The others filed right past the mural without even looking. Couldn't they see what he saw?

He grabbed Daisy's arm. "Look!" he said, pointing to the mural.

She turned her head. "So?" she said. "It's a painting of dogs playing poker. What about it?"

"It's a picture of my parents' village in Africa," Jesse insisted.

"Poker game," Daisy said.

"Africa," Jesse said.

"Poker game."

"Africa."

"Keepers!" Emmy broke in. "It's a blank wall. You're both seeing things that aren't there. Beware."

Uh-oh. We are in big trouble now, Jesse thought. He led them onward into a small circle of pillars, each one—like the one he had seen earlier—having a lifelike face carved into it. The first one Jesse came to was a woman with curly hair poking out from beneath the bill of a baseball cap. When he saw the curl in the bill and the team logo on the front of the cap, he gaped. It was his mother's lucky Boston Red Sox cap, the one she always wore—with her lab coat and scrubs and her bright red high-top sneakers—whenever she went to work in the clinic. As he watched, the eyes of the statue widened, and then the face smiled. Jesse pointed at her and stuttered, "M-m-m-m—"

The statue's mouth opened and spoke: "Oh, Jesse, baby! Daddy and I have missed you so much. You need to come back to us. Aunt Maggie called, Jess, and do you know what she said? She said you and Daisy have been fighting and you need some time apart. She says you've been a rude and sullen kid lately—a real junkyard dog. Nobody's blaming you, Jess. You're just homesick. I hate to say I told you so, but didn't I tell you this would happen, sooner or later?"

"N-n-n . . . w-w-w—" Jesse still couldn't get a single word out. All he could think was *How did my mother get down here?*

Ignoring his distress, Jesse's mother went on. "I know you've done your best to make this crazy arrangement work, and you've done a great job so far. But it couldn't last, don't you see? Daisy is a growing girl. She needs some girlfriend time. So does Emmy. Emmy's reached the age when a he-Keeper is really inappropriate. She needs a she-Keeper now, not you. But *I* need you, Jess, so come home. Now!" Two arms poked out from the stone and reached for him as if she wanted to draw him into the stone with her and back to Tanzania.

Jesse turned to Daisy. "Is it true?" he asked.

"Is *what* true?" Daisy looked at him strangely.

"Please explain why we have stopped again," said Emmy.

"My mother," he said, pointing to the statue.

"What?" Daisy asked in utter bafflement.

"My mother just told me you're sick and tired of me visiting and you need girlfriend time!" he said, his voice tightening. "She said Emmy needs a she-Keeper and now I can't be her Keeper anymore."

"How could your mother be down here? And how could she know about Emmy?" she said irritably. "Jesse Tiger, what in the Sam Hill are you talking about?" The tips of Daisy's pointy elfin ears were an angry red.

"My mother is here," Jesse insisted.

Daisy stamped her foot impatiently. "We don't have *time* for this, Jess," she said. "Look around you! Can't you see what's going on!"

While they had been arguing, the pillars had gradually moved closer together. Now not even Daisy could fit her body through the spaces in between them. "We're trapped!" she said.

But Jesse was determined to get Daisy to see what he saw. He gestured toward the pillar. "Why don't you ask her yourself."

"Fine!" Daisy barged past him and squared off with the statue. Jesse was wacky. Not only was this not her aunt Judith, Jesse's mother. It wasn't even a woman! It was clearly a man . . . with a spiky beard and a dapper bow tie. Daisy's eyes widened and her voice dropped to a whisper. "Professor Andersson? Is that you?"

She reached up and touched the face. It came to life beneath her hand.

"Thank you, child. It is, indeed, I," said the stone lips of the professor.

"Really?" she said to him.

"Would I lie?" he said.

"We're stuck in this circle," she said. "Professor, please, tell us, how do we get out of this maze!"

"I'm afraid that's not possible, my girl," said the professor.

"Why not?" Daisy asked.

"This plan of yours has roundly backfired. I appreciate the effort you have made to free me, but once again, you have placed your dragon in the path of gravest peril. And you have no one to blame but yourself."

"Oh!" was all Daisy could say. Her lower lip was trembling so badly, she couldn't speak.

The professor went on. "I suspect that Jesse, if given half a chance, would have come up with a far more prudent plan. But you never give him a chance, do you? That's because you have a fatal flaw: you are incapable of listening to others. Because you are incapable of real sharing. Real sharing requires heart, and that, dear girl, you are sadly lacking. Jesse has heart to spare, and that is why he is the real Keeper, and you, I fear, are merely an interloper."

"Stop it!" she burst out.

"Stop what?" Emmy asked in a small voice. "Jesse, Daisy, get ahold of yourselves, please?"

Tears stung Daisy's eyes. "Can't you see the professor?" she asked Emmy.

Emmy shook her head sadly. "No," she said. "I see nothing. I see a stone pillar and nothing more."

"It's not stone. It's the professor. And he says I'm heartless and a bad Keeper. Is it true, Emmy?" she asked.

"No. You have a very warm heart and are a very, very, very good Keeper," Emmy said. "Plus you have been very patient with my being such a snapdragon. So I will try to be patient with you and Jesse while you forget to use your brains."

"Why do you like Jesse more than me?" Daisy pressed on. "Is it because he's the one who found you? Is it because he's the one who named you?"

"No, Daisy Flower," Emmy said. "I chose you both because I like you both . . . the best."

Jesse shouted at Emmy. "No, you don't! You want a she-Keeper! I'm *inappropriate* now that you have wings!"

"Jesse, Daisy, listen to me," Emmy said. "Stop this!"

"Why don't you just admit it!" Jesse shouted. "You like Daisy more than me!"

Daisy shouted over him. "Come on! We all

know you like Jesse more. That's why you spoke to him first from inside your thunder egg! Did you call out to Daisy Flower? No, you called out to Jesse Tiger! Because he's a boy, and you like boys better!"

Emmy shook her head violently. "No, no, no, no, no! I can't listen to much more of this," she said, backing away from both of them.

"But you slept in her sleeping bag last night. Why not mine?" Jesse asked.

"Because Daisy doesn't kick in her sleep," Emmy said.

"I don't care what anybody says, I'm not going back to Tanzania. I'm staying in Goldmine City and fighting for my rights as a Dragon Keeper. Emmy, Daisy, you guys can't do this to me." Jesse's voice cracked. "You can't shut me out. Being a Dragon Keeper means *everything* to me!"

Jesse and Daisy stood toe-to-toe, their fists clenched. Then both of them burst into tears.

Emmy said, "I'll just leave. Maybe Mr. Wink will let me back into the Scriptorium, and I can dust the books and tend the stacks and wait for my mother to find me . . . *if* she ever finds me . . . and if she doesn't, I guess I will just be an orphan, a dragon without a Keeper, the saddest creature in all the domains." She heaved a shaky sigh and slipped easily between the pillars.

Daisy stopped crying and wiped her face on her sleeve. "No, don't, Emmy!"

"I am leaving you now," said Emmy. "Farewell, my Keepers."

"Don't leave, Emmy!" Jesse called out to her.

Together the cousins grabbed her tail and tugged.

"We're sorry!" Jesse said. "Please stay."

"You have to!" Daisy begged. "It's not safe for you alone."

Emmy was just opening her mouth to reply when they heard the sound of stone grinding against stone just overhead. A panel in the ceiling slowly opened and captured Emmy in a stark rectangle of light. Instantly turning sheepdog, she began barking ferociously at whoever was up there.

"Come back here, Emmy!" Jesse and Daisy whispered loudly, crouching behind the pillars. "Hide!"

But Emmy stood her ground, even when a giant white net swooped down and swept her up into it. The cousins lunged forward to grab the net, but the pillars held them back. They watched as the net rose swiftly above their heads and the stone panel ground to a close.

For a few moments, they stood and looked at the ceiling, as if they expected it to open again and return their dragon to them. When it didn't, Jesse said: "What just happened?"

"Somebody just stole our dragon," Daisy said.

"No, I mean *before* that," Jesse said. "What happened?"

"Hey, you two!" a familiar voice called. Daisy heard it, too, and they both looked around for its source. They found Uncle Joe's face in the nearest pillar. "Yeah, I'm talking to you two!"

Daisy's heart skipped. Her father looked angrier than she had ever seen him.

"All right, you two clowns! Turn around and march right out of here, double-time! Get your tails back home and consider yourselves grounded, both of you, for the rest of your natural-born lives!"

"Yikes!" Daisy cowered behind Jesse and whispered, "Poppy's hopping mad."

"Don't even try to hide from me," her father said. "This is private property you're trespassing on, and what did I tell you about that? This is not your castle to storm."

"I'm sorry, Poppy!" Daisy crept out from behind Jesse and approached the statue.

"No!" Jesse said, pulling her away. "Don't listen to him."

"That's Poppy, Jess!"

"No, it isn't!" He flung aside his glowing stone

and seized hold of her elbows, fixing her with a fierce stare. "Think about it for a minute, Daze. How could Uncle Joe be down here?"

Daisy hesitated and shook her head. She didn't seem to have a good answer.

"How could my mother be down here?" Jesse pressed on.

Daisy blinked and recovered her senses. "You're right, Jess. That's ridiculous. She's a gazillion miles away in Africa."

Jesse went on. "And the professor—"

"He can't be down here. We both know he's up in the tower," Daisy said.

Jesse nodded. "All this stuff we've been seeing and hearing, Daze, none of it is real. It's all some kind of a trick. This place," he said, hugging himself as the temperature plummeted even lower, "is under a spell."

Daisy nodded slowly. "Then all this fighting . . ."

"Is just a bunch of bad magic. Sadie Huffington put a spell on this place. And that hole in the cliff face we saw when we first got here? That *was* a doggie door. That's how she lures dogs down here and scoops them up in her net. It's a dog trap."

Daisy looked around warily. "And now it's a dragon and people trap, too."

The pillars were moving even closer together, a

crowd of stone faces bearing down on them, all of them talking at once: Mrs. Nosy-Britches screaming for the police; Jesse's mother coaxing him home; Uncle Joe bawling them out; the professor whispering evil things; Aunt Maggie lecturing them about getting along; Ms. Mindy scolding them for letting Emmy get caught; and even Mr. Stenson, the nicest guy in the world, reproaching them for getting dog slobber all over one of his "all-time fave books."

It wasn't until Daisy clapped her hands over her ears and started humming loudly, frost forming on her eyebrows, that Jesse knew exactly what to do.

He spun Daisy around and reached into the zipper pouch of the backpack, locating exactly what he knew they needed.

He spoke above the din: "This is what Miss Alodie meant when she talked about a *cold spell*. She sure enough didn't mean the weather," he said as he fitted one set of magic earmuffs around Daisy's head and the other around his.

CHAPTER NINE

STORM THE CASTLE

Silence. Jesse heaved a huge sigh of relief.

Daisy's eyes lit up with surprise. "Hey! I can't hear them anymore, can you?" she asked.

Jesse shook his head and smiled. "But I can hear you, loud and clear. Can you hear me?"

"Yep," Daisy said. She held her elbows and shivered. "Boy, that was one mean cold spell, wasn't it, Jess?"

Jesse nodded. "I think it's on its way out, though."

Sure enough, as if someone had switched on a furnace, the air in the chamber began to warm up. It even stopped smelling quite as bad.

Daisy took a step closer to Jesse. "I'm sorry I said all those rotten things, Jess," she said in a low voice.

"I'm sorry, too," he replied. "But it doesn't matter. We need to get out of this maze and into the castle."

"We're Dragon Keepers?" Daisy asked, holding out her fist.

"Dragon Keepers united forever," Jesse said, bumping her fist with his.

When they looked around, the circle of angry ranting pillars had vanished. And so had the maze. Before them lay a perfectly straight passageway, lit by torches, at the end of which rose a set of stairs, hacked into the stone wall in a crude zigzag.

"Just like Balthazaar's map!" Daisy said, tossing aside her glowing stone and smacking the notebook in triumph.

"Do you think it was here all the time and we just didn't see it?" Jesse asked.

"Do you think the earmuffs made the maze and all those crazy grown-ups go away?" Daisy asked.

"Maybe," said Jesse. "Or maybe it happened when we stopped fighting. Let's never do that again, okay, Daze?"

"Okay," Daisy said.

"So what are we waiting for?" Jesse said, sweeping an arm toward the stairs. "After you?"

"After you!" replied Daisy, dipping into a deep curtsey.

"Let's go together," Jesse suggested, and offered her his arm.

Daisy accepted it. "Let's go get our dragon back," she said.

"*And* the professor," Jesse added.

They marched down the passageway and up the stone stairs. Where the stone stairs ended, a wooden ladder stood bolted into the wall leading to a hatch in the ceiling. The cousins paused at the foot of the ladder while Daisy consulted the notebook. "According to this, the ladder leads to a trapdoor located just behind the receiving platform in the throne room."

Jesse nodded. "I'll go first," he said. "Unless you'd rather . . . ?"

"Please, be my guest," Daisy said.

Jesse climbed up the ladder, carefully raised

the trapdoor, and poked his head out. He saw the elegant purple and gold brocade backs of what looked like two thrones, one large and the other slightly smaller. Turning his head the other way, he saw the crest of St. George the Dragon Slayer, red on a field of white, emblazoned on an enormous banner hanging from a long golden rod suspended from the very high ceiling.

He was just about to climb out the rest of the way when he heard the distinct *scritch-scratch* of claws on stone. He turned his head slowly back toward the thrones.

"Um, Daze?" Jesse whispered, moving nothing but his lips. "Do me a favor? Hand me a couple of Miss Alodie's Rock-'em, Sock-'em Dog Biscuits."

"Would you say this is a 'dire' circumstance?" Daisy called back to him. "Because remember what Miss Alodie said."

Along the wall, he saw a giant dog shadow coming nearer. "Pretty dire, yeah," Jesse said.

"Coming right up," said Daisy.

Jesse felt Daisy place three of the moon-shaped dog biscuits in the palm of his hand. One second later, a Doberman pinscher with a choke collar as thick as a towing chain poked its muzzle around the corner of the throne. One look at Jesse and it bared its teeth and let out a snarl.

"Nice doggie," Jesse said in a trembling voice.

"Just remember," Daisy whispered frantically. "It's easy! So long as they know who's Top Dog!"

"Right," Jesse said slowly. It was hard to feel like Top Dog when your head was sticking up out of the floor like a pork chop on a platter. The dog lunged at him.

Jesse flung a biscuit at it. The dog caught the biscuit in midair—and then the most wonderful thing happened! The Doberman fell to the floor as if struck by lightning. It rolled over onto its back and stuck all four paws up into the air. Jesse waited a moment, and then risked crawling out of the hatch the rest of the way.

Very slowly, he walked over to the Doberman and stood over it. He gave it the best version of the patented Ten-Yard Stare that he could muster, but the dog didn't seem to need it. It made a pitiful mewing noise in the back of its throat, its tongue rolling out the side of its mouth. It seemed to want Jesse to scratch its belly. Jesse was pretty sure this was one guard dog that was now off duty.

"Hey, Daze! Come on up!" he whispered loudly.

By the time Daisy joined him, Jesse was on his hands and knees rubbing the dog's belly and cooing "good dog" to him.

Daisy stared down in utter amazement. "Wow,

Jesse, you really *are* Top Dog," she said.

"Don't you feel kind of sorry for him?" Jesse asked, giving the dog one last good scratch and getting up to leave.

"I feel sorry for him because he's under Sadie Huffington's spell, not because he got goofy from Miss Alodie's biscuit," Daisy said.

Jesse nodded thoughtfully. "You're right, I guess." Then he turned to an imaginary camera and said, "Well, that's all for this time. We'll see you next time, and until then, always remember, you *are* Top Dog if you act like Top Dog!"

"Oh, brother!" Daisy said, rolling her eyes.

As they made their way through the throne room, Jesse's eyes took in the rich carpeting, the iron chandelier the size of a large upside-down tree hanging from the ceiling, and the giant tapestry on one wall. The tapestry showed the scene of a lion being ripped apart by whippets while a knight, who looked an awful lot like St. George, watched in obvious satisfaction. Along the opposite wall was a wooden table as long as a bowling alley set with a silver bowl the size of a water trough.

"This place is awesome," he said to Daisy.

"Awesomely *hideous,* more like." Daisy glanced down at the notebook. She looked up and pointed to the doorway ahead, flanked by two highly polished suits of armor, complete with long axes. "The gallery should be straight through there, past those empty suits of armor," she said.

They were just passing through the doorway when one of the suits of armor creaked to life. A voice bellowed from behind the visor: "Halt!"

The long axes came down, slicing through the air behind them and only just missing them.

Jesse and Daisy froze. Then Jesse felt something poke him in the middle of the back.

"Forward, march!" the knights shouted, prodding them into the gallery with their long axes. The cousins stumbled forward.

"They're taking us to Sadie Huffington," Daisy whispered, then yelped as one of the knights jabbed her extra hard.

Larger than the throne room, the gallery was long and empty. Black and white squares of marble covered the floor. Lines of towering, fancily framed portraits stared out from the walls. The people in them all looked like they had lived in different time periods. As Jesse marched past them, he realized that every single portrait was of either George or Sadra. It would have been funny if it hadn't been so creepy. In a few moments, he'd be standing in front of Sadie Huffington, in the flesh. *Think of something!* he told himself. *Fast!*

He became aware of something in his hand. He looked down and saw that he still held two of the dog biscuits. He glanced back at their captors. He couldn't see their faces through the holes in their visors. Were they dog-men, just like the landscapers Daisy had described? It was worth a try.

"Mmmm!" he said loudly, smacking his lips. He opened his hand, which was sweaty and made the aroma of the dog biscuit more pungent. He held up his hand and waved it back and forth over his head, under the knight's noses.

"What are you doing?" Daisy whispered.

Jesse whispered back, "I'm tempting them with treats."

Daisy, catching on, began to play along. "Mmmm!" she said loudly. "I wish I had one of those tasty biscuits for myself."

"No way!" Jesse told her. "These tasty biscuits are all mine!"

The knights came around and stood in front of Jesse.

"Thanks, fellas," Jesse said, bringing the biscuits to his mouth. "Just what I needed! A snack break." The guards snorted and sniffed inside their helmets.

Jesse moved the biscuits back and forth an inch or two away from the two visors. Armor creaking, the knights' heads tracked the biscuits. Now holding a biscuit in each hand, Jesse moved a treat toward each visor and then quickly pulled it away. He did this until the dog-knights couldn't stand it a minute longer. They flipped open their visors and showed their human faces, their tongues hanging down to their chins.

Jesse picked the most eager-looking dog-man and stared into his eyes, never letting his gaze waver. When Jesse was sure he was Top Dog, he said in a sharp, firm voice, "Sit!"

Armor screeching, the knight lowered himself onto the black and white tiles, sitting down with a loud *clank,* never taking his eyes off the biscuit.

Jesse said, "Beg!"

"That's mean," said Daisy.

"It's not," Jesse said with steely calm. "I'm just showing him who's Top Dog. It's necessary."

With more clanking, the knight got up onto his knees and placed his armored gloves together beneath his chin. His mouth fell open and his tongue hung out as he slobbered and panted in anticipation.

"Good dog!" Jesse said, and tossed him the biscuit. The dog-man caught it in his mouth and crunched it up, then fell over onto his back with a noisy clatter, his arms and legs sticking straight up in the air.

Then Jesse went through the same routine with the second dog-knight. In short order, he had both of them on their backs, as meek and helpless as a pair of toppled tortoises.

"Sorry I can't stop and scratch your bellies, boys," Jesse told them.

"That was close," said Daisy. She turned and offered Jesse the backpack. "Better get out some more of those things. And snap them in half. There are an awful lot of dogs in this castle, and we need those biscuits to last."

Jesse took out the tin and started snapping the half moons into quarter moons while Daisy pored over the notebook. Jesse held on to a handful of biscuit bits and packed the tin away.

Daisy turned around and pointed. "Those twisty stairs?"

Jesse nodded at the spiral staircase made of wood that wound its way around a wide stone pillar in the center of the gallery.

"They lead to the big tower," Daisy told him.

A second later, two beefy German shepherds trotted down the stairs. Spotting the cousins, they launched themselves into the air and landed on the floor, heading for Jesse and Daisy at a dead run.

"Quick, Jess!" Daisy cried.

Jesse dropped down and skidded two dog

biscuit bits along the tiled floor like hockey pucks. The shepherds slid to a halt, scarfed up the biscuits, then promptly rolled over onto their backs with their eight paws in the air and their two tongues lolling out of the sides of their mouths.

"I wonder how long the effects last," Daisy said.

"Let's hope long enough for us to free the professor," Jesse said. They grabbed the dogs' front paws and, as gently as they could, pulled the dogs across the floor and hid them beneath the stairs.

Then Daisy and Jesse started up the spiral staircase. The wood creaked beneath their feet. Moving to the inside of the stairs, the cousins hugged the center pillar and found a less creaky way up. As they edged around the last turn, they saw the door to the tower room standing ajar. They heard Sadie Huffington's laughter ring out harshly. They crept closer and dropped to their knees, poking their heads around the edge of the half-open door. Jesse's chin rested on the crown of Daisy's head.

Sadie Huffington stood before a full-length gilt-framed mirror, wearing her Balthazaar of Belvedere coat. One pale hand gripped the choke collar around Emmy's sheepdog neck. Ms. Huffington was saying, "It turns out I won't be needing your questionable services any longer, Lukas. Now that I can add this furry specimen to my canine collection."

The professor's voice said in reply, "You might be holding that dog, but she is certainly not in your collection."

Jesse scanned the room, searching for the professor, but couldn't make out where he was.

Ms. Huffington said with a cold laugh, "Finders keepers. I caught her in my trap and scooped her up. And how lucky for me that I did. Because, you see, I know who she belongs to, Lukas."

Sadie Huffington held up Emmy's purple Great Dane–sized collar, its gold locket swinging. "A golden locket on a dog collar. A most unusual canine accessory, even by my standards. The locket contains the photographs of two children. I have seen these two children, Lukas. They came to call on you after I had . . . *persuaded* you to join me here. They are the Dragon Keepers of Emerald of Leandra!"

The professor replied blandly, "You *persuaded* me of nothing. I came here of my own free will."

Tapping the top of Daisy's head, Jesse pointed to the mirror.

Light from a small iron chandelier made it difficult at first for Daisy to see into the mirror. Then she nodded vigorously when she finally saw that in place of where Ms. Huffington's reflection was the professor. The professor was literally *in the mirror*. The poor professor! He was a prisoner times two: trapped in the tower and trapped inside the mirror!

"I intend to force their dog to lead me to them," Sadie Huffington said.

The professor chuckled. "Oh, that remains to be seen."

"You question me? I, who have dominion over all canine kind! Already she kneels before me and heels and begs and does my bidding. She'll lead me to the children. The children will lead me to their dragon. And when I have my way with the dragon, she will lead me to my consort."

The professor laughed out loud. "You are neglecting one crucial detail. The dragon doesn't *know* where your precious George is . . . any more than I do," he said.

Sadie Huffington's knuckles whitened as she twisted Emmy's collar. "Of course she knows. She's a dragon," Huffington said. "She knows all."

"I keep telling you, my dear, but you seem disinclined to heed me: *Emerald knows very little*. She's a useless hatchling. Her magic is latent— years and years away from being active."

Emmy began to whine as Ms. Huffington's hold on her collar tightened. "I have heard differently," she said. "I tell you, by moonrise, I will have the dragon in iron chains and my prince by my side. We will make our kingdom here, in this little hamlet in the shadow of the mountain. From here our power will grow and flourish."

"Perhaps," said the professor coolly. "But then again, perhaps not."

Jerking Emmy's collar so hard that she let out a yowl, Sadie Huffington quickly whirled away from the mirror and the cousins scooted into the shadows behind the door. Ms. Huffington stormed out of the tower room and stalked down the stairs, dragging a whimpering Emmy behind her.

Jesse grabbed the back of Daisy's shirt and kept her from leaping out into the open. They waited until they were sure that Ms. Huffington wasn't coming back. Then they tumbled out from behind the door and went to huddle before the mirror.

"Hey, Professor!" they whispered, waving to him.

The professor whispered back, "Hello! There you are! I knew I saw you peeping out from behind that door. At first I thought it might have been a pair of errant little palace Pekingese, but I should have known that it was my brave Dragon Keepers! I knew you'd find a way inside the castle!" His smile, beneath his new spiky little beard, was warm and kind, not at all like the sneaky, mean version they had met in the maze.

Daisy couldn't resist telling him in a loud whisper, "Emmy got her wings!"

"You don't say!" the professor whispered back, looking truly impressed. "Miracles continue to abound in this dragon of yours. It explains all that snapdragon moodiness."

Jesse and Daisy both nodded intently.

"Does Sadie really believe Emmy's a dog?" Jesse asked, still whispering.

"She does, indeed, my boy! Emmy's masking spell is one of the most powerful I have ever encountered," said the professor. "We must use this to our advantage. One of the few we can claim at the moment."

Jesse rummaged around in the backpack. "We have this, too," he said, holding up the Toilet Glass to the mirror.

"Ah! Very good!" the professor said approvingly. "I see you have also found your way into the Scriptorium!"

The cousins nodded enthusiastically. Jesse wanted to tell him all about the elf hole and Willum Wink and Balthazaar, but he knew this was wasn't the time or the place.

The professor said, "Sadie Huffington would

love nothing better than to reclaim this little bauble. The one thing our princess loves above all else is her face, in a mirror, and preferably one that lies."

"Does this mirror lie?" Daisy asked. Then she remembered her amazingly beautiful reflection. It had been too good to be true. "I guess you're right," she said, disappointment tugging at her. "Some trick."

"You may offer it up to her," said the professor. "But only here, in this room, standing before me. Am I understood?"

"I guess," Jesse said slowly. "But why?"

"Magical triangulation," the professor said.

"Right. Okay," the cousins muttered together, neither of them having the slightest idea what it meant, but sensing its importance.

"So should we stay here with you and wait until she comes back?" Daisy asked.

The professor shook his head. "She'll not be returning to this room any time soon. Let us say that she has exhausted her use of me. Her immediate plans lie elsewhere. The next time she returns will be to smash this mirror to kingdom come and destroy me."

"No!" Jesse and Daisy cried out, springing toward the mirror and pressing their palms to it.

"Shh," said the professor, finger to his lips. "The sentries will hear you. If you'll put your eye to the squint hole there, you'll see for yourselves."

It took Daisy a moment to remember what a squint hole was: a long vertical slit in a castle wall through which people of old used to look to see their enemies approaching.

Daisy and Jesse snuck over to the squint hole. Daisy put her eye to the bottom of the slit. Their current enemies, two enormous, shaggy black guard dogs, paced the ramparts just outside. She stood aside to let Jesse have a look. Jesse's eye widened. He turned back to her. "Tibetan mastiffs, all right," he whispered, swallowing hard.

They scuttled back to the mirror.

"It was not my intention to make you more fearful. Merely appropriately cautious," said the professor. "You have everything you need to fend off those brutes—as well as all the others. Now you must find a way to trick Sadie Huffington into coming back here. Clever Keepers like you should have no problem with that."

The cousins sat back on their heels. "That means we need a new plan," Jesse said out of the corner of his mouth, just the way he would have had they been in front of the computer.

Daisy nodded. Rescuing the professor wasn't

going to be quite as simple as they had imagined.

The professor continued. "Might I suggest that your first priority be to liberate Emerald? I fear that inhumane collar will inevitably goad her into making a most untimely unmasking. Look there." He pointed behind them.

Daisy and Jesse turned and looked over their shoulders to a mosaic on the tower wall. It showed a unicorn being lassoed by a gleeful blond knight on a white steed. (St. George, *again*!) The unicorn had a fat pearl embedded in the middle of its forehead.

"If you'll press the pearl in that noble creature's head . . . ," the professor said.

"What will happen?" Daisy asked, turning back to the mirror. But the professor was no longer there. All they saw were their own reflections—a couple of puzzled, slightly grubby-looking kids—staring back at them.

"It's nice to know that even when he's a prisoner, he can still come and go like that," Jesse said sourly.

"Typical," Daisy said with a snort. She got up and sneaked over to the unicorn mosaic, careful to keep her head below the level of the squint hole. Reaching up, she pressed the pearl. A panel swung open with a soft creak.

CHAPTER TEN

THE BEWITCHED HAMBURGER

Jesse and Daisy leaned through the passageway and looked in. Shafts of sunlight shone through a series of squint holes, lighting the way down a set of curving stairs. When the wall panel began to swing shut, the cousins jumped into the secret passageway. There was nothing for them to do now but go wherever the stairs led them.

Jesse stopped at a squint hole partway down and peered out. The courtyard below was empty. He had a clear view beyond the walls out to the lilac trees, where their bikes were stashed near the cul-de-sac. A couple of older boys were skateboarding in a lazy circle. Those young men were going about their normal, everyday lives while in the castle, witches and Dragon Keepers were waging a battle to the death. Jesse shivered. *Stop being so dramatic,* he told himself. *It won't help.*

"Come on!" Daisy whispered, tugging at his hand. Jesse nodded and tore himself away from the view.

When they got to the bottom of the stairs, a life-size metal statue of a peacock stood in their path. A sapphire was set in the eye of its centermost tail feather.

Daisy looked to Jesse and raised one eyebrow. He shrugged, so she pushed the blue stone. A second panel swung open before them. The cousins stepped through and found their noses pressed to the back side of a vast, rather dusty tapestry.

"We're back in the throne room," Jesse whispered in Daisy's ear. She nodded.

They linked hands and edged along the wall behind the tapestry until the toe of Jesse's sneaker stuck out from behind the frayed corner. Jesse knelt down and peered out. Now it was Daisy's chin digging into the crown of Jesse's head.

At least fifty dogs of all shapes and sizes but mostly big—and nearly as many hefty dog-men—milled about in a throng before the receiving platform, growling and panting and sniffing each other's butts. Sadie Huffington sat high on St. George's throne. With one hand, she grasped Emmy by the choke collar. With the other, she whipped her switch in the air to signal silence. Emmy didn't move, even as Ms. Huffington clipped the tip of one of her ears. The dogs below abruptly pointed their muzzles toward the Top Dog and sat on their haunches.

"My dogs, my strays, my curs, my faithful hounds and servants, two- and four-legged slaves, one and all!" Sadie Huffington's voice echoed in the great room. "The time has come for which I have been waiting, lo, these many years! The time for my reunion with my lord and my master, my consort and my lover, my handsome and brave one: St. George the Dragon Slayer!" She raised the switch and the crowd sat up and barked with obedient enthusiasm. Emmy, Jesse was pleased to notice, held still and did not join in.

"He is somewhere nearby; I feel him," said Ms. Huffington. "And this craven canine *here*," she said with a yank on Emmy's collar that made her yelp, "will lead me to him. Once we are joyfully reunited, my prince and I will return in triumph to the castle, mark my words, this very night! But we will not come alone." Her yellowish eyes widened and her voice dropped to a hushed pitch. "We will have in our possession a fresh young dragon with which to celebrate our reunion. And I promise you, there will be a bloodletting as in days of old! Yes, my faithful curs!" she cried out, gesturing toward the silver basin on the table. "The dragon blood will flow, and your faithful services to me will not go unrewarded! You shall have tender dragon bones aplenty to gnaw upon tonight!"

The crowd yipped and yapped and howled with glee. Jesse felt Daisy's fingernails digging into his shoulders. He reached up and held both of her hands in his, worried that she might burst from behind the tapestry and launch a running attack on the queen. Then suddenly, above the din, Jesse heard a sound that was different from all the others. Up on the platform at Sadie Huffington's side,

Emmy stood, head lifted high, baying in protest. Louder and louder, more and more insistently, she registered her objection to the Huffington plan.

Gradually, the noise of the dogs and dog-men fell away. Now that Emmy had everyone's attention, her baying sharpened to a shriek. The shrieking, in turn, grew in intensity until, for the first time in his life, Jesse knew the meaning of the term "ear-piercing." Dogs and dog-men alike shrank into themselves and protected their ears as best they could. Jesse pressed his own hands over his ears. Then Daisy pulled Jesse's hands away and he felt something blessedly soft muffling the sound. The shrieking, though still audible, now ceased to pain his eardrums. Jesse looked up and gave Daisy a grateful look for remembering Miss Alodie's ear-muffs.

The dogs in the crowd were not so lucky. They were now keening in agony. Even the powerful Sadie Huffington was writhing in pain. Flinging aside her switch and Emmy's collar, she ground the heels of her palms into the sides of her head. A line of bright red blood trickled from one ear.

Finally free, Emmy pawed off the choke collar. She shook herself briskly and then leaped from the platform. Continuing to emit the same intolerable shriek, she ran about among the crowd and, as if she were setting into motion a hundred-odd tops, dogs and dog-men began to spin in her wake, the dogs chasing their tails, the men reeling in place in frenzied circles. Around and around they all spun like a troop of whirling dervishes, all in the same direction, faster and faster and faster, a blur of fur and flesh and flesh and fur and, finally, all fur.

Abruptly, the shrieking stopped. After a few moments, Sadie Huffington opened her eyes and dropped her hands from her ears. Her eyes, bloodshot and bewildered, darted about the audience. The dogs and the dog-men had all stopped spinning at once. But something had happened to them during the spinning. Every single one of them, dog-men and dog, had been transformed into an English sheepdog, identical to Emmy! In desperation, Sadie Huffington scanned the fuzzy white mass in search of the one English sheepdog she needed above all else to get what she wanted.

She reached up and tore at her flaming tresses. "There is only one explanation for this kind of trickery!" she screamed. "Dragon magic!"

From behind the tapestry, Jesse and Daisy stared in mute astonishment at the heaving, yelping sea of sheepdogs in the throne room. Then, unseen by the others, one sheepdog broke loose and ran over to the tapestry. She nosed her way underneath and pounced upon her Keepers joyfully. Jesse and Daisy hugged Emmy and buried their faces in her fur.

"We're sorry we let you get dognapped," Jesse said to her.

"Let's go show the professor that we got you back," said Daisy.

The cousins and Emmy made their way along the wall behind the tapestry until they found the open passageway. Sidestepping the peacock, they took the stairs at a run. Halfway up, they heard the unmistakable sound of very big dogs snuffling and panting in the stairwell above.

"The mastiffs! They're headed our way!" Daisy said.

The three of them raced back down the stairs and managed to push the sapphire button and close the panel door behind them just as they heard the *thud-thud* of big dogs heaving their bodies against the door. By the time the three of them had wriggled free of the tapestry, the throne room was empty. They ran into the middle of the room and halted.

"If we go to the tower room, Sadie will follow us, and then we'll have her where the professor wants her," Jesse said.

"Perfect triangulation," Daisy agreed. "To the gallery!"

"To the gallery!" Jesse joined in.

Emmy barked in agreement, and they ran through the throne room and into the gallery. They were halfway across the chessboard floor when they spied Sadie Huffington near the top of the spiral staircase, her hairy horde howling at her heels. Ms. Huffington pulled up short when she saw them and swatted the railing with her switch. "Get them!" she cried as she and her canine troops poured down the spiral stairs.

"Scratch that plan," Daisy said as she frantically scanned her notebook.

"Where to now, Daze? Quick!" Jesse said.

Emmy let out a few anxious yodels to let them know that Ms. Huffington and her mob were nearly upon them.

Daisy flapped one nervous wrist while she tried to make sense of the plans, and then waved toward the back of the gallery. "Go! Go! Go!" she yelled.

They ran across the gallery toward a door sandwiched between two portraits, plunged into a long, dark hallway, and ended up in the scullery, the castle's vast kitchen area.

A pack of hair-netted lunch ladies were carving

up rare roast beefs and turkeys and unpacking dozens of bags of groceries in preparation for the night's feast. They stopped and looked up with dull curiosity, their tongues hanging out of their mouths.

"Excuse us, dog-ladies," said Daisy as she led the charge down the main aisle.

"Sorry to bother you," Jesse said as he ran past them.

At the back of the scullery, they came to a plain set of wooden servants' stairs, which they scrambled up, Emmy now in the lead. Behind them, Daisy heard a commotion in the scullery as their pursuers came crashing through.

The stairs led to one of the two smaller towers. The tower had two doors. One was locked. Emmy pounced upon the second one and it banged open onto a wooden rampart. They ran out onto the rampart.

"Look!" Jesse shouted, pointing down through one of the murder holes. "Emmy's spell is wearing off."

In the courtyard below, some of the sheepdogs were in the process of turning back into their true breeds, shaking themselves briskly. Still others were turning back into dog-men, climbing up from all fours. When they came to their senses, they took up the nearest garden tools—rakes, trowels, axes, and spades—and, brandishing them, turned around and headed back into the castle.

"Quick!" said Daisy to Jesse. "Get the thermos!"

Jesse pulled the thermos out of the pack.

"Pour the tea down through the murder hole!" Daisy shouted.

"Cool!" said Jesse.

"Great plan!" Emmy said, for now that she was outdoors, she was once again in dragon form. Far from being frightened, she was enjoying herself.

While Jesse unscrewed the lid of the thermos, Emmy said to her Keepers, "Did you see the trick I did back there in the throne room? Wasn't it beautiful?"

"Yes," Daisy said, "but I wish it had lasted longer. We need to find a way to keep these guys off our tails. Any ideas?"

"Watch this," Jesse said as he tipped the thermos into the murder hole. As the heads of the dog-men passed beneath it, Jesse dribbled a bit of the valerian tea onto the backs of their necks. One after another, they keeled over onto the ground.

"Still has a good kick to it!" Jesse said.

But their victory was short-lived, for the next minute, Ms. Huffington called out from the tower room they had just left behind. "We've got them now!"

The cousins and Emmy ran along the rampart toward the second small tower. But before they reached it, a band of angry armed dog-men burst through the door. Emmy, Daisy, and Jesse ran the other way but scooted to a halt when they saw that they were surrounded on both sides.

"Quick!" said Emmy. "Get on my back!"

Jesse and Daisy clambered onto Emmy's back just as her wings exploded open with a neat *pop-pop*. The purple-green wings unfurled as Emmy leaped into the air and glided off over the ramparts, well over the heads of their pursuers.

"This is preposterous!" Sadie Huffington shrieked, shaking her fist as Emmy swooped overhead. "Hatchlings can't fly!"

"Can, too!" Emmy called down to her.

"Cannot!" Sadie Huffington countered.

"Says who?" Emmy taunted.

"Says I!" said Ms. Huffington.

"What do *you* know?" said Emmy. "You're just a cranky old hag who's in love with the tanner's boy."

That last dig found its mark. Sadie Huffington sputtered in fury.

Daisy tapped Emmy on the neck. "Stop being such a tease and fly us over to the big tower!" she said.

"Wait!" said Jesse. "First do a couple of turns

around the courtyard! There are some majorly big dogs down there." He pulled the tin of biscuits out of the backpack. There were at least a dozen large dogs milling around below, looking up at them with hunger in their eyes.

"You guys want a snack?" Jesse shouted down at them. "Well, help yourselves! Bombs away!" He threw a fistful of biscuit halves down. The big dogs leaped into the air like trained dolphins and caught them in their teeth. Almost instantly, they dropped to the earth and rolled over onto their backs, motionless except for their lolling tongues.

"Save some of those for the Tibetan mastiffs," Daisy reminded him.

"Don't worry, I will," said Jesse.

Emmy flew over the ramparts toward the big tower. The two mastiffs burst out of the tower room and howled up at them, shaking their enormous shaggy heads as if already tearing their prey to shreds. Emmy hovered just over their upturned jaws while Jesse emptied the rest of the tin. The mastiffs immediately fell into a big black heap of snoring fur.

Just outside the door to the tower room, Emmy touched down on the ramparts. Jesse and Daisy scrambled off Emmy's back and ran inside.

Even with her wings collapsed, Emmy was too

big to fit through the doorway, but she squeezed in as far as her shoulders. "Hello, Professor!" she said to the mirror. "Come out of there and see my beautiful new wings!"

The professor greeted her with a jovial laugh. "Emerald, you are a constant marvel!"

"You always said I was precocious," Emmy said.

"Let me see!" said Jesse, consulting his wristwatch. "Triangulation should be achieved, Professor, in about . . . two minutes."

"When she gets here, Jess," Daisy said to Jesse, "beware the patented Ten-Yard Stare."

"Are you kidding me?" Jesse scoffed. "She doesn't stand a chance with me. Haven't I proven that I'm Top Dog?"

"I guess," said Daisy, mustering her hope.

Exactly a minute and a half later, Sadie Huffington stalked up the stairs and slammed into the tower room.

"Ah!" she said as her yellow-green eyes came to light upon Jesse. "We meet again, my little pet."

Jesse's arms flopped to his sides. "Hi," he said faintly.

Daisy's hopes faded as she watched Jesse's eyes turn all glassy.

"Because you've been so good, I've brought you

a treat," she said to Jesse, as if they were the only two people in the room.

Daisy smelled it before she saw it. The next moment, Sadie Huffington brought out from behind her a big, fat, steaming double cheeseburger. Daisy didn't even like cheeseburgers, but this one smelled delectable. And hamburgers were practically *the* reason Jesse had wanted to live in America. Next to bush-burgers, they were, hands down, his favorite food on the face of the earth.

"Don't eat it, Jesse Tiger!" Emmy warned.

From the mirror, the professor called out, "Danger, Jesse. Danger. It's a bewitched hamburger that you see before you."

That hamburger held Jesse's attention like nothing Daisy had ever seen. He licked his lips and his throat worked, as if he were already swallowing his first bite.

"Sit," Sadie Huffington commanded, holding the hamburger just over his head.

Jesse sat on the floor, eyes on the hamburger, which was running with savory juices.

"Beg," she said, a sly smile twisting her face.

Jesse got up on his knees with his hands dangling beneath his chin.

"Good dog!" Ms. Huffington crooned. She

pinched off a piece of the hamburger and tossed it to him. Jesse caught it in his mouth and chewed it up.

The next moment, Daisy cried out. In place of her cousin, a small, scruffy brown mutt eagerly awaited his next taste of the bewitched hamburger, his little whip of a tail slapping the floor.

"No!" Daisy yelled. She didn't want a dog for a cousin.

"Heel!" Sadie Huffington said, snapping her fingers and stomping her boot heel.

Jesse's little claws scrabbling on the stone floor, he got up and went to her obediently. She tossed him another morsel. He caught it and chewed it up and licked his whiskery chops.

"Sit!" she commanded.

Jesse sat at her feet and looked up at her, anticipating the next luscious morsel of bewitched hamburger. But the hamburger, which Ms. Huffington now held ever so casually in one hand, inches from his shiny black nose, was too tempting for the poor little fellow. With a furtive movement, Jesse took a tiny nip of it. Quick as a rattlesnake striking a mouse, Sadie Huffington smacked his muzzle. Jesse yelped.

"Dumb mutt. No more treats," Ms. Huffington said to Jesse. Then she looked up, as if noticing

Emmy, Daisy, and the professor for the first time.

"Ah! How convenient for me to have you all in one place . . . to dispense of all at once. Into the mirror you'll go, and then I'll smash it to smithereens. All except for the dragon, of course. The dragon is mine."

"You only wish!" Emmy said with a snort.

Ms. Huffington's yellow eyes narrowed. "You, my hatchling, are far too full of yourself. But I'll fix that." She cracked a cruel smile.

"What will you do?" Emmy asked. "Turn me into a dog?"

Daisy was frantically trying to catch Jesse's eye. With all her powers of concentration, she directed the patented Ten-Yard Stare at the little pup's big brown eyes. But it was no use. He wouldn't meet her gaze. His attention appeared to be elsewhere. She turned around. He was looking at Emmy and Emmy was looking at him, giving him her own very special version of the Stare.

"Fetch the backpack, that's a good Jesse-dog," Emmy told him in the gentlest of voices.

Daisy made it easier for Jesse by letting the backpack slip off her shoulders and drop to the floor. Jesse trotted over and picked up the backpack strap in his teeth.

"Bring the backpack to me," Emmy said.

Jesse dragged the bag over to Emmy and stood away from it, wagging his proud little whip of a tail. During this time, Ms. Huffington appeared to be frozen, either from magic or simply shock, Daisy couldn't tell.

"Very good!" Emmy said. "Now open the backpack."

Just as Emmy the sheepdog had done for Jesse the boy at the library party, Jesse the dog now used his paws and his doggie teeth to pull the tab of the zipper on the backpack.

"Very good. Now, can you find Sadie Huffington's gift?" Emmy asked. "Find the gift, Jesse!"

Jesse stuck his muzzle in the top of the backpack and snuffled around. Meanwhile, Ms. Huffington stirred to life.

"A gift?" she asked. "For me?" All of a sudden, she looked very pleased and very greedy.

"It would be rude of us to come to your castle without bringing a hostess gift," Emmy told her.

Jesse held the silver compact in his jaws, his tail wagging proudly.

"What a good little dog you are!" Emmy said. "Bring the gift to the nice lady, now." Then, from between her clenched teeth, Emmy said to Daisy, *"Nobody calls my Jesse-dog dumb and gets away with it."*

Jesse took the compact to Sadie Huffington, who snatched it from his jaws. Jesse yelped and ran back to stand beside Emmy.

"My Toilet Glass!" Sadie exclaimed with delight. "Wherever has it been all this time!"

"That would be telling, wouldn't it?" said Emmy, suddenly sounding very grown-up and very sly.

They watched as Sadie Huffington opened the silver compact and held the mirror up to her face. She sighed with pleasure.

That was when Emmy's irises began to spin like a set of brilliant green pinwheels. Her nostrils gave off three peppery pink puffs of smoke, which rose to the ceiling and filled the room with a purplish vapor. "*Switch witch!*" she whispered.

CHAPTER ELEVEN

THE RESCUE

The very next instant, the compact clattered to the floor next to the heap of Balthazaar's coat, which no longer appeared to have Sadie Huffington inside it.

At the exact same moment, Jesse turned back into a boy. Daisy didn't know whether to pat her cousin on the head or throw her arms around him and hug him, she was so glad to see him in boy form once again. So she did both, saying, "Welcome back to the human race, Jess." Then Daisy turned to Emmy and asked, "Where did Huffington go?"

"Into the Toilet Glass. I flushed her," Emmy said with an impish grin.

"I feel a little sick," Jesse said, clutching his stomach.

"Don't fret, my lad. The effects of the be-witched hamburger will wear off in no time," said Professor Andersson, stepping out of the mirror as casually as the rest of us exit from a bus.

Daisy was quite taken aback to see him in person. She had always thought of him as being a towering figure, but he was actually a wee elfin slip of a man, no taller than Jesse.

"Thumping good dragon magic, Emerald!" said the professor.

Emmy smiled modestly. "Slight variation on tri-angulation. Mirror spell combined with switching spell. Easy as cake."

Easy as pie, Daisy nearly said. But it seemed petty to correct the dragon who had just pulled off such excellent magic.

Daisy knelt by the coat and picked up the Toilet Glass. She looked in the mirror. There was

Sadie Huffington, looking every bit the witch, making terrible angry faces at her. Daisy shut the compact with a shiver.

"Can she get out?" Jesse asked uneasily.

"No way," said Emmy. "She's stuck like goo."

Jesse grinned happily, and so did Daisy. "Goo" seemed like the perfect word for Sadie Huffington's fix. "Check the pockets of the coat for Emmy's collar," he said.

Daisy found it tucked in one of the big pockets. "Whew!" she said, holding up the collar and kissing the locket. "My mother would have *killed* me if I'd lost this." Daisy reached up and fastened the collar around Emmy's neck.

"Balthazaar is going to jump for joy when he gets his skin back," said Jesse.

"Exactly," said Daisy.

"That's a sight I'd like to see," said the professor with a chuckle.

Then Emmy said sadly, "But what about me?" Her eyes traveled from Keeper to Keeper. "There will be no joyful jumping for me—not until I find my mother."

"Emmy," Daisy chided gently, "we can't just leave this place. We have to help all these poor bewitched dogs and dog-men get back to their normal lives."

"Don't concern yourselves with them," the professor said with a blithe wave of his hand. "I will take care of everything here. You three run along and do what needs doing. I'll see you back on the Web." The professor strode to the door.

"Wait," Daisy said, holding out the Toilet Glass to him. "Can you take this, please?"

"Oh, dear me, no. That's for your collection. I'd say you've won the witch's head, fair and square," he said, and he disappeared with a jaunty wave.

Giving the Toilet Glass a last wary look, Daisy put it in the backpack.

Jesse shrugged. "Hey, maybe it will come in handy," he said, "like for scaring away rabid rats." Then he looked at his wristwatch. "It's almost dinnertime."

"Keepers!" Emmy said, her eyes growing stormy. "You promised—after we freed the professor, we would look for my mother."

Daisy looked at Jesse. "She's right, Jess."

"I know . . . but Uncle Joe will be expecting us for dinner," he said uneasily. "I keep remembering how mad he was down in the maze. I'd hate to make him that mad for real."

"We'll stop by Miss Alodie's and call Poppy," Daisy said, "and tell him she invited us over to her place for dinner."

"And then she'll feel like she has to feed us. Something really *weird*, no doubt," Jesse said. "Hey!" he said with a sudden look of relief. "I think I might be getting hungry again! Is there anything in the backpack?"

Daisy shook her head. "I'm afraid our picnic lunch got a little smashed. We'll grab a bite to eat at Miss Alodie's and then go track down Emmy's mother," said Daisy. "Plan, Emmy?"

Emmy heaved a sigh of satisfaction. "Thank you, Keepers. Now, come out of this tower and climb on board Air Emerald." She backed out the door and onto the ramparts.

"Emmy," Jesse said sternly. "No flying. We're *walking* home. Riding, I mean. We left our bikes outside, and besides, we can't just go flying around in broad daylight. Someone will see us and report a UFO or launch an antimissile attack on us or who knows what? And, in case you haven't guessed, I've had enough excitement for one day."

Emmy shook her head fondly. "Jesse Tiger, can't you guess? Dragon magic will whisk your bikes back home and make us all invincible."

"*Invisible,* don't you mean?" Jesse said. "Whoa. First I'm a dog and then I'm invisible. Cool!"

Jesse got down on the floor and rolled up

the dragon coat, but it was too bulky to fit into the backpack, so he held it under his arm.

Then Jesse and Daisy joined Emmy on the ramparts and climbed onto her back. With a great flap of her wings, they were aloft.

Jesse started to make a joke about being *dog* tired, but the joke died on his lips as they rose higher into the air. To have flown in the Scriptorium was one thing. To fly above a place he had known all his life was something else altogether. It was as if the entire town had all become a vast and intricate toy set, spread out on a quilt in his bedroom. Jesse shouted to Emmy, "Can we take the scenic route, please?"

Emmy nodded and banked to the left. In seconds, the town was behind them. They skimmed over barns and silos, sheds and chicken coops. Jesse wanted to lean over, reach down, and pick up each shiny tractor and truck, brush his palm across the ripening tops of the cornstalks, stroke the miniature black-and-white cows with a pinky. And all the while, he felt a wide-open singing feeling inside of him. For the first time, he didn't feel afraid. It was as if his whole life, he had been a little bit scared about *something*, even when he didn't quite know what that something was. And right now, he wasn't afraid of *anything*. Maybe Emmy had used the right word earlier. Maybe, for a moment at least, he really was *invincible*.

"Ta-da!" he shouted, raising both arms high in the air.

Daisy looked at him and smiled happily, as if she knew exactly what he was feeling.

Before long, Emmy was soaring over the familiar rooftops of Goldmine City. She flew right above Main Street, where the people were shopping, going home from work, driving their cars, and not a soul looked up at the sky. No one saw them flying overhead, thanks to dragon magic.

Soon the roof of their own house came into view, along with the steel corrugated roof of the garage and the much smaller, bright orange roof of Uncle Joe's Rock Shop. Was Uncle Joe inside? Would he ever in a million years guess what they were doing at that very minute?

Emmy coasted over the front yard and down their street to the end of the block, coming in for a landing where Miss Alodie was polishing an emerald-green reflection globe. The globe stood at the end of a long rectangle of gleaming white stones running like a stripe down the center of the yard. Both globe and stripe were new additions to the back garden.

"There you are!" Miss Alodie called to them. "I don't know when I have seen a more handsome set of wings, Emerald! When they told me you were cross and crabby, I knew there was a good reason for it. I was so sure you were fledging that I prepared a landing strip!"

"Thank you, Miss Alodie," Emmy said. "It's beautiful."

"You're just in time for high tea," said Miss Alodie.

"Do you want to come in for something to eat?" Jesse asked Emmy as the cousins followed Miss Alodie into the cottage.

"No, thank you. I'll just pop over the fence and hunt up a tasty tidbit or two," said Emmy.

"I knew it!" Daisy whispered furiously to Jesse. "She's going to feed on defenseless woodland creatures."

Jesse shrugged. Having experienced firsthand, even for a very brief period of time, what it was like to belong to another species, he was not inclined to be critical. Besides, he was so hungry himself, woodland creatures sounded a lot more filling than what Miss Alodie was whipping up for them in her kitchen at that very moment. They plopped down on the couch.

"So," Jesse asked Daisy, "what was I like?"

Daisy wrinkled her nose. "What do you mean?"

"What was I like when I was a dog?" Jesse said.

Daisy smiled and shrugged. "Snakes and snails and puppy dog tails. About what you'd expect. Oh, and I was right."

"About what?"

"You were a mutt," she said.

"Was I a big mutt or a little mutt?" Jesse asked. "Short-haired or long?" For some reason, he really needed to know what kind of a dog he was.

"Let's see. You were about the size of a beagle. You had shaggy fur like an Irish setter. A skinny little tail like a whippet. Floppy ears like a spaniel, and the sweetest little plump muzzle sprinkled all over with white freckles. You were completely *adorable*. If I'd seen you in a cage at the pound, I would have taken you home like that," she said with a snap of her fingers.

Jesse didn't know whether to be flattered or insulted.

Just then, Miss Alodie came out of her kitchen with a tray of food, which she set down on the tea table in front of them. Daisy picked up one of the triangles of bread and bit into it. "Delectable!" she pronounced.

Jesse picked up a triangle for himself and pulled the bread apart. It looked like some sort of red jelly. He slapped it shut and nibbled one corner. It tasted spicy, like his father's aftershave. He took a few more nibbles and then washed it all down with a glass of mysterious-tasting juice.

Miss Alodie sat in the chair across from them and slapped her knees. "Tell me *everything!*" she said eagerly.

Between bites of aftershave sandwiches and sips of mystery juice, Jesse and Daisy told her of their adventure. They finished by showing her the coat and the Toilet Glass.

Miss Alodie took particularly wicked delight in seeing Sadie Huffington trapped inside the mirror. "Who's Top Dog now?" she asked, thumbing her nose at the furious little face.

Jesse took the mirror back and shut it tight, because it was clear that the miniature Huffington was cursing them all something fierce, and it made him feel a little jumpy.

"I'm not crazy about the idea, but we're supposed to add this to our Museum of Magic collection," Jesse told Miss Alodie. "Oh, and can you guard Balthazaar's coat until we get back?"

"Of course I can," said Miss Alodie with a wink. "I promise I won't let *this* one get away."

"And can you call Poppy and tell him we're staying for dinner?" Daisy asked.

"I hope he won't be too mad at us for waiting until the last minute," Jesse said.

Miss Alodie ruffled his hair and made him feel a little like a puppy again. "I promise you, he won't mind a bit. In fact, he has wanted to take Maggie out to that new Japanese restaurant in town," she said with a twinkle in her eye. "And now he'll have the perfect chance to do so."

Miss Alodie walked them out into the backyard, where Emmy waited for them by the gazing globe.

"Can we fly to the Dell?" Daisy asked.

"You bet," said Emmy. "The sooner the better."

"But it's only a short distance," Miss Alodie said. "Just because you have a dragon who flies now doesn't mean that you two should stop making use of your legs."

"We promise to walk just as much as before," Daisy said. "But today we'd really like to get a close-up look at the weather vane on top of the dairy barn, wouldn't we, Jess?"

Jesse nodded. For nearly every summer of their lives, they had sat in the heifer yard next to the barn and stared up at the weather vane of the horse galloping whichever way the wind blew him. "When we learn to fly," they had promised each other, "we'll soar up there and—*whoosh!*—

make that horse gallop wherever *we* want him to go."

The cousins climbed onto Emmy's back and the dragon took off, flying over the neat row of backyards on their block until they reached their house. There she swooped over the laurel hedge and down into the great green bowl of the pasture. The old dairy barn loomed ahead. The sun setting behind the Deep Woods made the shabby roof shingles look like pure gold.

Emmy was just homing in on the weather vane when she stopped short in midair and craned her neck downward. "Jesse! Daisy! Look!" she called out to them in a hushed voice.

The big red book was laying facedown, draped over the ridge of the barn roof.

"Mother!" Emmy said.

At the sound of Emmy's voice, the red leather covers rose an inch or two and then dropped again, as if they were too exhausted to do anything more.

"It's me!" Emmy tried again. "Your daughter: Emerald of Leandra!"

At this, the covers of the book did a little flip. The book lifted itself and flew up level with them. Book and dragon fluttered in the air before each other.

"You look tired, Mother," Emmy said gently. "Come with me."

Emmy led the Book of Leandra, gliding downward across the pasture. Dragon and book landed side by side in the softest, greenest part of the pasture between the barn and the brook.

Jesse and Daisy climbed off Emmy and stood back as Emmy went to her mother. "Isn't this better than that rough old rooftop?" she said kindly. "Have you been up there all this time? I'm sorry I kept you waiting, but we've been very busy."

Daisy felt Jesse tugging on the sleeve of her shirt. She tore her eyes away from the touching scene.

Jesse said, "Sorry, but I really think we should give them some privacy, you know?"

"Oh!" said Daisy, blushing to the tips of her ears. "Of course, we should. Sure."

They slowly walked away, Daisy stealing an occasional look over her shoulder. They went into the barn and haggled a bit about where exactly on the Museum of Magic table to place the Toilet Glass. Jesse thought the animal skulls would make excellent sentries. But Daisy felt the Sorcerer's Sphere would exert greater power. Jesse finally gave in and agreed to place the Sorcerer's Sphere smack on top of the Toilet Glass. That way, the magic of the sphere would keep Sadie Huffington locked up good and tight inside the mirror.

"Can we go back outside now?" Daisy asked Jesse when they had completed their task.

Jesse nodded. "Sure," he said. "Let's see how the mother and daughter reunion is going."

They found Emmy hunkered down over the book, which now lay open, its pages tinged pink from the rays of the sun setting over the Deep Woods. Daisy and Jesse watched from a short distance away as the pages of the book fanned in front of Emmy's face. Whether Emmy was reading what was written on the book's pages, or listening to her mother, or simply absorbing through her magical scales all that had once been her dragon mother, who could really tell? But it was clear from the changing expressions on Emmy's face that she was having the experience of a lifetime. When at last the book snapped shut, there were tears pooled in Emmy's green eyes.

Daisy caught her breath when, in the next moment, the ghostly form of Leandra, a great, dark, red-scaled dragon four times Emmy's size, emerged from the book and enveloped Emmy gently in her wings, rocking her like a baby.

Now it was Daisy who had tears in her eyes as she watched Emmy discover what it was like, for the first time, to be held by her own mother.

Soon enough, Leandra evaporated into a cloud of dark red smoke and bubbled back into the book. Emmy heaved a great sigh and came to join Jesse and Daisy.

For the longest time, nobody spoke. The three of them stood in the pasture and watched the sun drop behind the trees and a tide of darkness steal over the pasture, leaving in its wake a damp green fragrance laced with late-summer wildflowers.

CHAPTER TWELVE

EMERALD'S TURN

At last, Emmy began to speak: "She wanted to be there when I hatched. So she checked herself out of the Scriptorium and went to the big, high mountain covered with snow. That's where she hid my thunder egg a hundred years ago."

"On High Peak," said Jesse, "where we found you."

Emmy nodded. "A hundred years ago, she had foreseen her own death. So she hid me there to keep me safe from the Dragon Slayer."

"She was a good mother," Jesse said.

"She was the best," said Daisy.

"But she arrived too late," Emmy said. "By the time she got to High Peak, you and Uncle Joe had already left, taking me home with you."

"We're sorry," said Jesse.

Emmy's eyes hardened. "But the Dragon Slayer was still there on the mountaintop," she said.

"And that's how St. George got her," Daisy said.

Emmy nodded sadly.

"How come she didn't just escape?" Jesse asked.

"St. George had once drunk her blood, and it gave him special power over her," said Emmy, wagging her head. "For the longest time, my mother said, she was senseless, trapped inside the book. After I hatched, her pages began to stir. I didn't know it then, but she began sending me messages."

"That's why you were always calling for your mother," said Jesse.

"And that's how I learned those spells. She was teaching me, even though I didn't realize it at the time. For a book, she is a very good mother."

"Yes, she is," Jesse agreed.

"The best," said Daisy again.

"She was very happy for a while at Miss Alodie's cottage," Emmy said. "She was still trapped, but at least she could see me when I visited her every day. But then I stopped visiting—"

"Because you stayed home to read your library books," Daisy said.

"Plus you were a junkyard dog," Jesse added.

"I was, wasn't I?" Emmy laughed softly. "Maybe it was just as well that I stayed away."

"But she missed your visits, so she went out looking for you!" Daisy said.

"Yes!" said Emmy.

Then Jesse said in a halting voice, "I guess it would have been better for you and for her if she had gotten there on time that day at High Peak. Then you'd have had your mother from the time you hatched, instead—instead of us."

"Oh, no, Jesse Tiger!" said Emmy, smiling sweetly at him. "Leandra was powerless against St. George. She never would have been able to protect me . . . not like my Dragon Keepers."

"Really?" Jesse asked.

"Truly?" Daisy asked.

"Really *and* truly," Emmy said.

Jesse smiled. Then Daisy smiled. At that moment, those were the exact words they both needed to hear.

Later that night, while Aunt Maggie and Uncle Joe were having their green tea ice cream at the Japanese restaurant, an airborne caravan took off from the new landing strip near the gazing globe. Miss Alodie, hugging Balthazaar's coat to herself while she rode on the Book of Leandra, let out a whoop of delight as they swooped through the air over the rooftops of the little houses below.

When the twinkling lights of the village of Goldmine City came into view, Daisy—sitting by Jesse's side on Emerald's broad back—pointed out the peaked roof of the public library. "What's that?" she asked as they drew closer.

There was a curious dark, rectangular groove cut into the ridge of the library's roof. It looked just like a slot in a giant mailbox, except that it wavered slightly, as if the roof were in the process of melting away.

Jesse called out to Miss Alodie, "What's that?"

Miss Alodie threw back her head and chortled. "I believe the Scriptorium is offering us a giant Chicken Box!"

From Emmy's back, the cousins watched as the

Book of Leandra swooped down into the slot. As the tip of Miss Alodie's beanie disappeared into the darkness, her voice echoed merrily back at them: "And now for a little nocturnal browsing!"

Emmy plunged in after Miss Alodie. Perhaps it was their double-dragon escort, or maybe it was the entryway, but that night's trip went much more smoothly than it had the night before. For one thing, they did not appear to need the Sorcerer's Sphere, even though they had remembered at the last minute to pack it. What was more, not a hair on Daisy's head was out of place. And no one felt the slightest need to scream.

As Emmy dived down through the bank of spicy-smelling fog, the aisles of the Scriptorium once more came into view, stretched out beneath them like a vast grid of streets, the stacks like rows of skyscrapers. But where were the shelf elves? Jesse expected to see the shelves swarming with elves, but there were none in sight. The next moment, he saw why.

Emmy sailed over the tops of the stacks toward the Recovery Laboratory, where a crowd of shelf elves, bibliotechnicians, and bibliotherapists had gathered in one great throng. The sound of their helium-high voices all cheering made Jesse want to cry (because he was touched) and laugh uproariously (because it was the funniest sound he had ever heard). He turned to Daisy and saw that she was feeling the same weird jumble of emotions. She squeezed his hand in excitement.

Emmy and Leandra landed on two adjacent worktables. The cousins climbed off their dragon and onto the floor. On a third tabletop sat the heap of parchment that was Balthazaar of Belvedere, his pages as tattered as ever and completely inert. Gradually, the cheering died away and the Scriptorium fell silent.

Miss Alodie hopped down from Leandra and bustled over to Jesse and Daisy. She thrust the black coat at them. "I think I'll let you two make the official presentation," she whispered, her blue eyes dancing.

The cousins each held one side of the rolled-up coat and were wondering exactly what to do, when a familiar figure elbowed its way through the crowd and stepped forward. He bowed deeply and then seemed unable to straighten himself up.

"Watch the back now, Mr. Wink," he said to himself as two smaller shelf elves hurried over. He smiled with blissful relief as they pulled him back up. "Forgive me. It seems my skeletal system is in need of a little elfiniotherapy. (Isn't it? It is!) Willum Wink, Chief Steward of the Shelf Elves, welcoming you back to the Scriptorium, Emerald of Leandra and her stalwart Keepers. And who else have we here? We are graced by your presence, Alodie the Elder. And Leandra of Tourmaline, you gave us all a terrible fright. I suppose you are aware that you are *eons* overdue? Techs! Techs!" he called out with a sharp clap of his hands.

A crew of eager blue-clad elves assembled themselves before him. "Give the Book of Leandra a thorough going-over, will you, and make sure every page is pristine and intact," said the Chief Steward.

The bibliotechnicians set to work, swarming over every inch of the Book of Leandra.

Mr. Wink turned to Jesse and Daisy. Eyeing their bundle, he said, "Is that what I think it is?" Without waiting for an answer, he turned and tapped the pile of parchment on the table at his back. "Oh, Balthazaar! Balthazaar of Belvedere! Yoo-hoo! Come out and see what these wonderful Keepers have delivered."

A cloud of dark gray mist bubbled up out of the pile of parchment and formed itself into the enormous ghostly black figure of the dragon. A deep voice rumbled out of the mouth of the giant apparition: "Well, well, well. I have to say, I never thought you'd pull it off."

The cousins unfurled the coat and proudly spread it out on the table. Balthazaar let out a long, low growl and turned to hawk a fiery wad of spit over his shoulder, sending elves skittering in all directions. "Look!" he said, his eyes flaring up like red-hot coals. "Look at what they *did* to my beautiful black scales, to my magic, my essence, my soul, my identity, my pride. *How dare they?!*"

"Easy, old-timer," said Willum Wink. "Don't work yourself into a lather. I've seen our recovery teams perform miracles. (And we're going to need one. Won't we? We will! It's unanimous!)"

Another hand clap from Mr. Wink brought on a troop of red-clad bibliotherapists, lined up and ready for duty. "See what you can do," Mr. Wink told them, "about restoring this defiled draconic epidermis to its former glory. I am hereby authorizing you to spare no effort, time, or expense."

"Well, now," the giant black dragon rumbled, turning to Jesse and Daisy. "Now that you have so easily produced one half of my skin, you should have no trouble getting me the other half in short order."

Jesse and Daisy turned and stared at each other in disbelief.

Daisy muttered to Jesse, "He's some piece of work, isn't he?"

Jesse agreed. "The *original* junkyard dog."

"It makes you grateful to be Keeper of a *nice, polite* dragon, doesn't it?" Daisy said.

"That's for sure," Jesse said.

Emmy cleared her throat and said, "Excuse me, my Keepers, but your *nice, polite* dragon is hungry again. I could use a couple of those tasty little Green Eggs and Hamwiches right about now."

"I don't know about the green eggs," said Daisy, pleased that no more defenseless forest creatures were on the wish list that night, "but I think we can manage the hamwich."

"Now that you mention it, Em," said Jesse, "I'm starting to feel a little peckish myself. What I wouldn't give for a tin of those crunchy, spicy dog biscuits!" he said, licking his chops and rubbing his paws together with glee.

Hearing this, Emmy, Daisy, and Miss Alodie exchanged looks of absolute mortification.

Jesse burst out laughing and pointed at them. "If you could see your faces! It was a joke, you guys. I'm back to being a boy again, I promise. But I'm a hungry boy, that's for sure."

"Then say good night to your mom for now, Emerald," said Daisy, "and fly us home."

"Plan!" Jesse and Emmy agreed.

And an excellent plan it was.

Dear Mom and Dad, The heat wave ended, followed by a brief cold spell, and now it's just right. Aunt Maggie has stopped talking about giving Emmy a haircut. She says she feels autumn in the air. I can even smell it. It smells like rotting fruit and wet leaves. Aunt Maggie says it's the scent called Back-to-School, which I am really looking forward to. It will be my first American Halloween, too! Daisy and I have even begun to plan our costumes. She's going to be a sheepdog. I'm not sure yet, but I think I'm going to be an elf. A shelf elf. Bet you don't know what that is. Well, I'll tell you . . . someday, when I have a ton of time. Right now we have to get some books back to the library before it closes. Only chickens use the Chicken Box, and one thing I'm pretty sure of is we're not chickens. Are you guys gonna come visit soon? Don't worry. I'm really doing great, but I miss you!

Lots of love, your son in America,

Jesse Tiger

In the little town of Sea Cliff, where KATE KLIMO grew up, the Stenson Memorial Library was just down the street from her house. She got her first wallet when she was eight, not for money, but to hold her library card. She can still remember exactly where on the shelves her favorite books of fantasy sat. In Middletown, New York, where she and her husband, Harry, raised their three sons, the public library is housed in a wonderful old former railway station—and from there, she and her family have taken many memorable trips.

Don't miss the Dragon Keepers' next adventure in The Dragon in the Volcano!

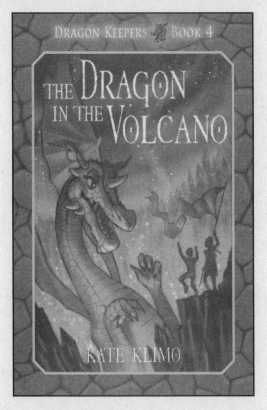

Turn the page for a sneak peek!

FROM

THE DRAGON
IN THE
VOLCANO

CHAPTER THREE:

HEADING FOR HOT WATER

Jesse, swatting at the smoke, said, "I get the feeling she isn't too happy with us."

Daisy wiped her watering eyes on her sleeve.

"Come on," said Jesse, looking warily about at the hundreds of thousands of volumes of retired dragons sitting on the shelves. "Time to go."

Willum Wink seemed to have returned to his duties, so they went back to where the ruby sphere sat on its giant golf tee. Daisy reached up and grabbed the orb.

Jesse craned his neck and stared upward. The center of the dome, where the Scriptorium exit was, was lost in the swirling mists above them. "How are we supposed to get out of here?" he wondered aloud, feeling a little dizzy. The last time, Emmy had flown them out.

Just then, Jesse felt a breeze riffle the hair on his forehead. The big red book came scooting down the aisle toward them like a magic carpet.

"Don't look now, Jess, but I think our ride is here," said Daisy.

"I guess she couldn't be *too* mad at us, after all," said Jesse.

The cousins scrambled on top of the book and held on tight to the ring as Leandra, in book form, whisked them up through the layers of golden fog, to the tippy-top of the dome. There Daisy popped the sphere into the exit hole. After a few uncomfortable moments of feeling as if they were being squeezed out of a toothpaste tube, they arrived back in the last aisle of the nonfiction section of the Goldmine City Public Library. They clambered quickly to their feet and dusted themselves off.

Daisy found herself nose to nose with a book on crystals and gems. "Well, what do you know?" She took the book down from the shelf and paged through it. "And it has awesome color plates."

They took Daisy's book to the front desk, where Mrs. Thackeray was still on duty. When she saw them, her eyes popped behind her rhinestone spectacles. "My goodness! The two of you look as if you've been dunked in glitter!"

Daisy laughed uneasily and handed her book to the librarian. She stole a glance at Jesse. He did, now that she took the trouble to notice, look as if he were glowing all over. She checked out her own hands and saw that they, too, shimmered as if she had dunked them into a bucket of mica.

They said so long and thanks to Mrs. Thackeray, and then they rode back home. After parking their bikes in the garage—cold and dank and dragonless as it was—they trooped up the back steps, through the mudroom, and into the kitchen.

The sight of Miss Alodie standing at the stove, in place of Aunt Maggie or Uncle Joe, caught them both off guard.

In a long, flowered apron, Miss Alodie turned and lifted a wooden spoon in salute. "Heigh-ho, cousins!"

Jesse wrinkled his nose. The kitchen smelled highly unusual, which, he supposed, was to be expected.

"You're just in time for dinner!" Miss Alodie said. Then she got a good look at them and set her wooden spoon down on the stove with a *thunk*. "Land sakes, cousins! You've been *dipped*!"

"In *what*, is the question," said Daisy uneasily.

"Why, in dragon dust!" Miss Alodie said. "What else?"

"I guess you could say that Leandra smoked us by accident," Jesse explained.

Miss Alodie shook her head slowly and firmly. "Keepers, I know accidents when I see them, and this was no accident."

"Anyway," Daisy said, "we're going up to the barn to return the Sorcerer's Sphere to the collection. Then we'll be right back to discuss our findings over dinner."

"Do we have to?" Jesse whispered to her on their way out the door. "Eat dinner, I mean."

"One moment, cousins!" Miss Alodie said. She was rummaging around in a floral-patterned carpet-bag. "I have something in here for you." She emerged with a flat, round canteen and handed it to Jesse. It was covered in what looked like purple dragon skin.

"What is it?" he asked.

"Keepers, it's clear to me you're headed for hot water," Miss Alodie said, her blue eyes steely. "This will come in handy."

"Thanks, Miss Alodie," said Jesse doubtfully.

Daisy turned around so that Jesse could slip the canteen into the backpack. The weird things Miss Alodie gave them always wound up being very useful.

"We'll be back soon," Daisy said to Miss Alodie as they headed for the back steps.

"Oh, I doubt that very much!" the little old woman called after them. "But don't worry. I'll see you when I see you."

When they got to the barn, Jesse took the sphere out of the backpack. It was once more a crusty old orb. Daisy watched to make sure he returned it to its place on top of the Toilet Glass. That was when she realized that something was again amiss.

"Hey, Jess," she said. "What's wrong with this table?"

Jesse stood back and scanned the objects on the table. His voice rose in alarm. "The horseshoes! *Where are the horseshoes?*"

Not just one but all four of the rusty horseshoes were now missing.

"Let's check outside," Daisy suggested.

They ran outside to where Emmy had set up the ringtoss game behind the barn. Sure enough, the four horseshoes were lying on the ground, two of them near the stake and the other two near the throwing line, all neatly arranged and facing in an easterly direction, as if they were on the feet of a giant, invisible horse.

Jesse knelt to pick up the nearest horseshoe, and when he did, a long brown hind leg appeared, then a switching tail, followed by a sleek, chestnut-colored haunch. Jesse straightened and stepped back. Soon the rest of the animal was visible: a big brown farm horse stood before them with its feet firmly planted in the horseshoes.

"It's Old Bub!" Daisy said, enchanted. "Just how I always imagined him, Jess!"

Old Bub flicked his long tail and plodded over to the tree stump. He stood there for a few moments, his tail swishing back and forth. Then he snorted and scraped the ground with his front hoof, twisting his head around and looking at them with one wise brown eye.

"Um, Daisy?" Jesse said. "I think he wants us to mount and ride."

Jesse boosted himself up onto the tree stump. The horse had no saddle, no stirrups, no halter, and no reins. Jesse grabbed a fistful of wiry mane and hoisted himself up onto Old Bub's swayback. Once settled, with one hand still twisted in the mane, he lowered an arm for Daisy, who had scrambled up onto the tree stump after him. She grabbed hold of his hand, swung herself up behind her cousin, and locked her hands around his middle.

The horse lurched forward, joints creaking and head bobbing.

"Whoa!" said Jesse.

The horse shuddered to a halt.

"What's happening?" Jesse said.

"You just said, 'Whoa,' Jess," Daisy pointed out, with a nervous giggle.

"I didn't mean it *that* way," Jesse said. "I meant it like 'Woweee!'"

"Yeah, well, Old Bub doesn't know the difference, do you, old feller? Let's try this." Daisy squeezed Old Bub's rib cage with her legs and said, "Giddyup!"

Old Bub started up again. Daisy let out a sigh of relief. Considering that the horse was so huge, it was nice to know they had a *little* control over him. Daisy had ridden horses before, but not many as large as this one, and none, of course, that were magical!

The horse was heading in an easterly direction down the winding barn road. Daisy, peering out from behind Jesse, saw something lying ahead of them on the road. It was a small white object.

"What's that?" she said, pointing.

As they came closer, she saw that it was a rolled-up pair of clean white tube socks.

"Socks . . . from Emmy's nest!" Jesse said. "Should we stop and pick them up?"

Daisy shook her head. "No, we'll pick them up later. If we get down now, we'll never be able to get back on again. Let's just find out where he's taking us."

The horse plodded on down the barn road and crossed the street. His heavy hooves clip-clopped loudly on the pavement, then became muffled again as he entered the woods on the far side. The cousins had never been in these woods before. Tall pine trees grew so close together that they blocked out the sun, tinged the air deep green, and filled it with the smell of Christmas. It wasn't long before they passed a ball of bright-red kneesocks.

Daisy said, "Wasn't *Hansel and Gretel* one of Emmy's favorite books when she was little?"

"Only after she got over being terrified of the witch in the woods and the kids in the cage, yeah," Jesse said.

"So are you thinking what I'm thinking?" said Daisy.

Jesse was silent for a bit. "You think Emmy's left a trail for us?" he asked.

"Socks instead of stones or bread crumbs," Daisy said, her heart quickening. "Let's hope."

As if Old Bub sensed her excitement, he switched to a trot. Daisy gripped Jesse, and Jesse gripped the horse's mane. Just as they were getting used to having their teeth rattling around in their heads, the horse lengthened his stride into a smooth canter.

"Woweeeee!" Jesse said.

Old Bub rolled up an old logging trail filled with ruts, which he rocked over with heart-stopping ease. The socks kept coming—dark blue, hot pink, argyle, striped, polka-dotted—one after the other, as Old Bub flattened his gait into a gallop.

Daisy's stomach lurched and her nose ran, but

she didn't dare let go of Jesse to wipe it. Daisy had been on a galloping horse for one or two breathtaking sprints, but this was a run that went on for so long that it wasn't possible to keep holding her breath. She was soon exhausted and panting, as if it were she and not the horse who was doing the running. And all the while, there was the steady *creak-creak-creak* of the horseshoes, like rusty hinges opening the door to . . . *who knew what?*

Suddenly, they plunged into deep shadow. Daisy looked up and gasped. Over the jagged treetops, the snowcapped mountain loomed, shockingly close and glowing pale pink in the rays of the lowering sun.

"Yep!" Jesse said, as if his suspicion was now confirmed. "That's where we're headed. High Peak!"

"Emmy's first nest," Daisy said, and a shiver of anticipation rippled through her.

The path grew steeper, and now the sock balls became single socks, stretched out like bright arrows pointing the way upward in the gathering gloom. The route they were on was familiar from hikes they had taken with Uncle Joe. Old Bub leaped up the steep paths with the nimbleness of a mountain goat.

Jesse lay along Old Bub's neck, arms grimly

tangled in the mane. Daisy clung to Jesse, her cheek pressed to his back. Beneath her interwoven fingers, she felt the wild beating of Jesse's heart. Daisy was sure her own heart was beating just as rapidly. What had been exciting was now terrifying. What if the horse's hooves slipped on the rocks? What if the two of them slid off his back? Would they tumble backward off the side of the mountain?

After a long while, the terrain began to level off a bit and the horse slowed to a trot. The wind pounded Daisy's back like icy fists and made her glad for her winter coat. She opened her eyes and looked around. The trees had dwindled to almost nothing. They were on the upper slopes of High Peak, above the timberline. It was a good twenty degrees colder up here. The wind whipped their hair every which way and worked its frigid fingers down the collars of their coats.

Jesse untangled his right hand from Old Bub's mane long enough to point to a group of boulders lying up ahead. This was the spot where Jesse had found the geode from which Emmy had hatched. But Old Bub lurched right past the spot and crunched up the snowy hillside toward the summit.

At the top of High Peak, there was a lake, no bigger than the pool of a large public fountain but much, much deeper. Uncle Joe always said that it was deeper than the highest skyscraper was high, because it was the water-filled crater of an extinct volcano whose core reached down to the magma layer beneath the earth's crust.

Old Bub stopped on the banks of the lake and, reminding Jesse of a bus that had come to the end of the line, released a long puff of steam and settled his body to say he was done.

The cousins gratefully slipped down from Old Bub's back. The horse wandered off and dropped his head to nibble at the blades of dull-green dried grass poking up through the snow. Jesse and Daisy staggered around, catching their breath, shaking out their limbs, and checking themselves for bruises.

Jesse stopped suddenly and looked at the lake. It was a body of water so freezing cold that nobody ever swam in it, even after a vigorous climb on the hottest day of the summer. In the last rays of the setting sun, wisps of steam rose off its glassy surface.

Daisy knelt, dipped a hand in the water, and quickly pulled it out. "It's boiling hot, Jess."

The cousins stared down into the water's crystalline depths.

"And look!" Daisy said, pointing. "See it? There's another sock . . . under the water." Shivering, Daisy straightened and stepped back.

Jesse went behind Daisy and unfastened the backpack. Daisy watched as he came around and unscrewed the top of the purple canteen. Throwing back his head, he took a healthy swig from it. At first, his face puckered up something fierce. Then his eyes popped open, his mouth gaped, and he began to pant.

"Jesse Tiger, what in Sam Hill are you *doing*?" Daisy asked, worried. "Are you choking? Can you speak?"

"What Miss Alodie said to do," he said between gasps. "This stuff is for when we run into hot water, which is exactly what we just did." He gestured at the steaming lake.